AUCTIONS AND ALIBIS

THE HEMLOCK INN MYSTERIES BOOK 1

JOSEPHINE SMITH

WESTERN COAST PRESS

For Max

A bead of sweat trickled down my back. A fly buzzed lazily around the room, drunk from the heat. I resisted the urge to lick the sweat off the top of my lip and tried to focus on my boss, who, based on the dark patches under his arms, was doing about as well as the fly and I were with this heat.

"Simone, enough is enough. I can't have this kind of drama in my place of business."

I tried not to roll my eyes at Antonio's overreaction—this place ran on drama, and Antonio seemed to stoke the fire whenever he could. I didn't want to even think about how I was going to tell my parents or Chrissy that I'd lost another job. Having two doctors as parents and a successful professor for a sister could really make someone question her life choices.

"Look, Antonio, I'll pay for the guy's drinks and apologize to his girlfriend. You're making a bigger deal out of this than you need to." Antonio was known for having a soft spot for his bartenders, particularly the newer ones.

He'd kept many bartenders employed longer than they

should have been, including Darla, who didn't know the difference between an old-fashioned and a mint mojito, but she had three kids at home and too many bills.

I didn't want to take advantage of Antonio—convincing him to hire me with no prior bartending experience, save for a love of gin and tonics and salty peanuts, had felt shady enough already—but maybe there was a way I could get out of this.

"You punched him in the face!" he said incredulously.

Maybe not. "Barely! Besides, he was twice my size. I figured he could take it." How was I supposed to know he was recovering from the flu and would fall like a house of cards after one punch? "Plus, look at what he was doing to his girlfriend."

I sat back in my seat, my knuckles stinging, as if chastising me for assaulting a sick man. Clearly, his sickness didn't stop him from roughing up his girlfriend near the bathrooms, and the three shots of tequila I'd dropped off twenty minutes before hadn't helped him either. It was hard to feel bad for punching a guy who was smacking on his girlfriend.

"I can't have my bartenders punching customers," Antonio said, shaking his head and grimacing. "It's not good for business."

I sighed as Antonio droned on about how sorry he was for firing me and how much he liked me and wished I could stay. The air conditioner unit in his office rattled in the corner, barely making a difference in the room.

For a bar owner, Antonio had a surprising number of books back here, and the book theme continued in the bar, with bookshelves lining the walls. He even had readings from local authors every Wednesday.

I'd thought bartending would be fun; an easy way to

pick up a few bucks after the temp agency stopped returning my calls. They were clearly still upset about the incident with the chickens, but it wasn't my fault the organic farm was really a front for smuggling drugs. How was I supposed to know the chickens would ruin the "merchandise" after I accidentally left a cage open on my way out of the office one night? The temp agency didn't want anything to do with me after that, and I had to wonder why they sided with the drug smugglers.

Instead, I'd ended up at Antonio's, which attracted struggling writers, who dominated the Wednesday readings with poorly constructed screenplays and stories that barely concealed their mother issues. Antonio's also managed to attract whiny customers who tipped like they saw us spitting into their drinks each night. I'd at least gotten overtime at the temp agency, but this bar was my only option right now.

As Antonio took a breath, I leaned forward and clasped my hands in front of me, putting on my best poor-me face. "Antonio, I'm sorry about what I did. I was just trying to protect that woman. You know how much I need this job."

Losing this gig and not being able to pay my rent would mean moving back home with my parents. While my mother was counting down the days until this happened, excitedly crocheting a new blanket for me every week, I was less enthused about that prospect.

"I'm sorry," Antonio said, shaking his head, his gaze down at his hands on the desk, his voice apologetic. "You know how much I like you, but I can't risk the liability. I need you to leave. Now."

~

"ANTONIO'S just worried about getting sued," Jill said to me on my way out of the bar, squeezing my shoulder. "You should know you did the right thing."

Marco, the other bartender on duty with us, pulled me into a hug. "We're going to miss you so much," he said, squeezing the breath out of me.

I pulled away from him, tears pricking at my eyes at the kindness these two were showing me. They'd been welcoming when Antonio first hired me, showing me the ropes and teaching me how to make a Manhattan, and even tried to convince Antonio to let me stay after I punched that scumbag. Would I find this amount of kindness at some other bar in Los Angeles? Not likely.

"Thanks, really," I said, slipping my shoulder bag over my arm, my brown cheeks flushing at my emotional reaction. I didn't feel like breaking down in a bar in the middle of the day.

They both gave me one more hug, then walked me out of the building. I waved goodbye and slid behind the wheel of my car, blinking away tears.

You ever have a day that's so bad, you start to wonder if the universe is out to get you? That it just wants to knock you on your face and dance around you in circles, laughing, and never once lending a helping hand? As I slipped on my seatbelt, my phone rang. Seeing my sister's smiling face on the screen, it would seem that, yes, the universe was out to get me today.

"Hey Chrissy, I was just thinking about you." I put the phone on speaker and pulled out of the bar's parking lot, the oppressive heat that had built up in my car weighing down on me like a blanket. "What's up?"

"What are you doing on Friday night? Do you still have that purple dress I bought you for Christmas last year?"

"Why?" I asked, my suspicion-meter perking up.

"A new lawyer started at Mark's firm this week," Chrissy said, not realizing that she was meeting all of my expectations in the worst way. "He's your age and new in town, and Mark and I thought it might be fun if you two came over for dinner. Hannah's staying with Mark's parents. What do you say?"

What I wanted to say was, never in this lifetime. But I kept my mouth shut. I loved my sister, and her husband, but their incessant desire to find me a man was wearing on me, mainly because their previous contenders had all been duds.

Mark was a great guy, but his firm seemed to attract lawyers who only knew how to talk about the law and didn't want to let anyone else get a word in edgewise. After the first dozen times learning what an abatement was, I might as well take the bar exam myself.

Plus, after my last relationship ended in cheating and screaming matches, I preferred to remain dateless for the foreseeable future. My thirties were the time for finding myself, right? Of course, I was still two years off from that particular decade, but, given my track record, I had a feeling I'd ride into that era single and with zero cares left to give. Or so I hoped.

"Unless you're working Friday? You're probably working Friday," Chrissy said, not seeming to question why I was silent. Shuffling on her end likely meant she was pulling out her planner. "What about Saturday? Or the next weekend? I think Dan's free most days."

I smirked. Of course he was. Never a good sign when a potential paramour is always available for dinner. Didn't Dan know anything about playing hard to get?

"I'm not sure what day I'll be free." I pulled into the

parking lot of my apartment building and switched off the engine. I'd always hated L.A. traffic, and I regretted coming back to my hometown a year ago any time I had to drive over two miles. Lucky for me, Antonio's bar was a simple five-minute drive from my apartment and didn't even require me to get on the freeway.

"Why?" Chrissy asked. "Is Antonio putting you on double shifts again? Do you want me to talk to him?"

I rolled my eyes and climbed out of my car. Antonio had only made me work a double once, and he'd paid me well for it, but my sister was now convinced he was abusing all his workers.

"No, it's fine." I walked into the lobby of the building and cursed the landlord for being too cheap to install AC. I had a few fans going in my apartment, lazily moving the hot air around. Hopefully, it would be more pleasant than this sauna.

"I got fired," I said, spitting out the words and climbing up the stairs to my third-floor unit. As a kid, I'd always preferred ripping off the Band-Aid, even if it made me cry. Apparently that childhood tendency hadn't gone away. Was that the reason I'd punched a customer earlier today?

"What? Fired? Why?"

I told her what happened, playing up my heroism and skipping the flu symptoms of the customer.

"Antonio can't just fire you! You were protecting one of his customers!"

"Yes, but I think assault on another customer is a fireable offense," I said, making it to the third floor and pausing at the top of the stairs to catch my breath. Every day, up and down these stairs, and I was still breathless when I made it to the top.

As Chrissy continued in my ear, asking if I wanted her to

talk to Mark and see if any of the attorneys at his firm would take on an employment case, I walked down the hall to my apartment, stopping with a jolt when I saw my front door.

"Chrissy, I need to call you back," I said.

The blue EVICTION notice stared up at me from the door. I clicked off my phone, ignoring her protests, and rested my head against the door. No job, about to lose my apartment, and a sister determined to find me a husband. What else could go wrong today?

I entered my apartment, tossing my keys on a side dish by the front door and moving into the kitchen to get some water. The two fans I had running weren't doing much to circulate the air. I glanced at my watch: three o'clock. The sun wouldn't be down for hours and I had nowhere to be. Would I melt into the floor?

I gulped down my water and headed into my bedroom, where I'd at least had the foresight to close the blinds before I'd left earlier. The room was marginally cooler than the rest of the apartment, and I fell back on my bed, staring up at the ceiling.

The eviction notice had said I had sixty days to leave the apartment if I couldn't pay the last two months' rent, which I couldn't. Sixty days to uproot my life and find someplace new to stay. While I didn't relish the thought of returning to my childhood bedroom, my parents at least had air-conditioning. It might give me some time to reflect on the past year and determine where, exactly, things had gone wrong.

My phone rang in my hand, jolting me out of my thoughts. I wasn't in the mood to deal with Chrissy right now. Instead, a random number appeared on the screen, and I answered the call, wondering if the universe was coming to kick me while I was down.

"This is Simone."

"Simone Evans? Daughter of Frank and Henrietta Evans?" the voice on the other end asked.

Odd way to introduce yourself. "Yes, that Simone. What's this about?" Someone calling to collect a bill, or maybe my kneecaps?

My stomach grumbled and my mind drifted to my fridge, which I knew had exactly one apple inside, plus half a pint of milk. At least I could say I had strong bones.

"My name is Ron Chapman. I'm calling regarding the estate of Sylvia Marks."

Aunt Sylvia's face flashed in my mind and I sat up in bed. I hadn't seen her in years. Who was calling me about her?

"What do you mean by *estate*?" I asked, fiddling with my bedspread.

"Well, I've got you written down as the main point of contact. I'm sorry to have to tell you. Your aunt has passed away."

A chill came over my body and my ears filled with a roaring. My mind felt sluggish, like it was climbing through oatmeal, trying to comprehend what this man was telling me.

How could she be dead? I'd just spoken to her... I counted in my head... eight years ago. A lot could happen in that time. The Hemlock Inn appeared in my head, a memory from my childhood. Chrissy and I had visited over the years when we were kids, running around the rooms like we owned the place. I was almost nine the last time we went, then the trips stopped suddenly, and we spent our summers at a camp in Los Angeles.

My phone calls to Aunt Sylvia had become less regular over the years, and we'd barely kept in contact after I turned eighteen. Birthday and Christmas cards, plus the occasional text message or voicemail to see how things were going.

Why hadn't we stayed in better contact? My mind flashed onto some fight between my mom and Sylvia, but I couldn't remember the details of what had happened between the two sisters, and this man on the phone was still chattering in my ear.

"I wasn't even aware she was sick," I said, guilt coursing through me. "How did she die?"

"Pancreatic cancer. It came on quick, and she had just enough time to get her affairs in order. I really am sorry to have to break the news to you," he said, his voice kind.

My guilt grew as I thought of Aunt Sylvia, alone, battling cancer. Uncle Tim, her husband, had passed away a few years ago.

"That's so tragic," I said, unable to find the words to express the guilt and sadness currently building in my chest. "Will there be a funeral?"

"Actually, she asked to have a small funeral," he said, "with only one other person in attendance, and she requested I wait to call the family until after she'd been cremated."

"That doesn't really surprise me," I said, cracking a smile. Aunt Sylvia had always hated having the spotlight on her and once told me when I was sixteen that she wanted to keep her funeral small and quick. Still, I knew my mom would be heartbroken to hear this.

"Well, thank you for calling and telling me," I said, my voice breaking over the words. A lump had formed in my throat and I took some deep breaths, trying to hold it together. I needed to get this man off the phone so I could call my family and give them the news.

Was this the ultimate punishment from the universe? Having to deliver this awful news to those closest to me?

"There's more," he said. "I'm in Pine Brook, up here in Washington state. I was hoping you could stop by the inn, so we could discuss the terms of your aunt's will."

Terms of her will? What was he getting at? "I'm not sure I understand what you mean. What will?"

A pause on the other end. "I see. It seems your aunt didn't tell you. She's left you the Hemlock Inn."

Aunt Sylvia left me her inn? This didn't make any sense. We hadn't spoken much these past few years, and I wasn't the responsible one in the family. Why would she trust me to take care of an inn?

Did I even want to take on the responsibility of an entire business? I could barely get through six months as a bartender. This was a lot more work than I was used to.

Then I remembered that I was jobless and about to be homeless. As I stared at the eviction notice still crumbled in my hand, an inn seemed like a good deal right now, though a part of me still wondered if I could handle it.

At the very least, it got me out of L.A. for a bit, while I tried to figure out what I was going to do next. Proceeds from selling the inn could be a game changer for me right now. I'd hate to disappoint Aunt Sylvia, but I'd be the first to admit I wasn't responsible enough to run a business like that.

"I can be there tomorrow," I told Ron, figuring I had enough in my savings for a plane ticket. Maybe the universe had decided she wanted to leave me with a few options, after all.

2

I landed at SeaTac International on time the next day, the only interruption to the smooth flight from some turbulence we hit passing into Oregon. I'd always been comfortable on airplanes, but you never know when it's going to be your last flight, so I gripped my armrests a little tighter and kept my gaze out the window. Soon, the tip of Mt. Rainier poked out of the clouds and my fingers loosened.

With no checked bags, I walked past all the other flyers milling about the checked bag pickup area and headed towards the rental car pickup. The blonde behind the counter frowned when she saw my sweater.

"You got a coat on you?" she asked as she swiped my credit card and passed me the keys.

I shook my head, pocketing the keys and signing on the rental agreement. The woman raised her eyebrows and pursed her lips, as if I'd committed some heinous crime by not bringing a coat.

Stepping out of the airport to pick up the rental car, I

realized why she'd made that face. The blast of cold, blustering air nearly sent me onto the nearest plane back to California. This was going to take some getting used to.

Wrapping my sweater tighter around my body, I hurried to the Honda the man at the rental desk pointed me to. I blasted the heat once inside and rubbed my hands together to warm them up.

Late September in Washington state was a different beast from the dry heat of L.A. this time of year. Good thing I wasn't planning on staying in Washington too long; just a couple days to sign the paperwork and find a buyer for the inn.

I'd leapt at the chance to escape from my problems in California when Ron had called, but even I knew I couldn't keep running from them forever. But picking up a winter coat might make these few days easier to get through.

Ron had told me to come straight to the inn, so I could drop off my stuff and stay there for the night. He said normally we'd be meeting in his office in Pine Brook, but he wanted me to see the place my aunt had left me before getting into all the estate details.

I remembered the inn always being full of people, the sun shining bright all day long, vibrant flowers adorning every surface of the inn. That image was not what I showed up to on that fateful Tuesday morning.

Ron had briefly mentioned during our call that the inn had seen better days, but I hadn't paid much attention. He'd said that Aunt Sylvia ran into trouble with the inn in her last few years of life and had already been thinking about selling it when she'd gotten sick.

The inn still drew a sizeable crowd in the warm summers, but once the weather turned, as it had this morning, the barrenness of the inn stood out. I peered through the windshield as the inn came into view.

Majestic, looming, and old. Those were the words that came to mind. The colors were dimmer, the flowers less vibrant, the sky gray. The driveway led to a curved entrance up front, and there was a parking lot in the back.

The line of tall pine trees bordering the inn drew my gaze. These might be where the town got its name from. The forest ran back about ten miles before you got to the next house. The eponymous brook ran through the woods and carried along small bugs that liked to nip at little girls' ankles.

A smile spread across my face as the memories transported me back twenty-odd years: running through the woods, wind whipping through my hair, chasing down Chrissy and playing knight and princess.

She always wanted to be the princess, and I happily took on the role of knight. I thought back to the scene at Antonio's bar and the tear-stained girlfriend, who hadn't looked all that sad when her boyfriend went down. Maybe I had picked up a thing or two from playing knight as a kid.

The inn was Tudor-style, with dark wood, a sloped roof, and an arched entryway. Greenery ran up the side, with a brick pathway and a flight of stairs leading to the front door. Pine trees framed the building, and the windows were arched. A chimney poked into the sky, tufts of smoke pumping out.

My feet crunched through leaves as I walked up the pathway, and the wind whistled through the trees in the back. Birds cawed in the distance but, besides the sound of my breathing, all was silent.

Surprisingly, the inn was quiet as I entered with my

rolling suitcase. When I was a kid, Aunt Sylvia had always talked about the importance of greeting guests as soon as they arrived, so I'd expected a bellhop to rush out as soon as I'd pulled up to the inn. I supposed times had changed.

The lobby was empty, although it was as I remembered it: dark paneling on the walls, high ceilings, and so many windows. A fire crackled in the fireplace across the lobby, and my breath caught in my throat at the sparkling chandelier hanging from the ceiling, just like it had back then, except with a few dead bulbs now.

A man walked across the lobby from the door that led to the back offices. He was short and stout, and several years older than me, with pale skin, graying hair, and eyes that creased when he smiled. This must've been Ron.

"Ms. Evans, thank you so much for coming by," he said.

I shook his outstretched hand, wondering how few guests the inn got that he could recognize me on sight like this.

We chatted about the weather and my flight, and, rather than leading me back to the office area, as I expected, he took us out to a courtyard nestled in the middle of the building.

The courtyard was roofed to protect guests from the rain, but the ceiling was made of glass. This space would be glorious in the spring, when the sun shone brightly, but today the gray skies lent it a more subdued atmosphere. I did spot some vibrant flowers scattered throughout the courtyard, though.

Ron led us to a grouping of outdoor chairs and a settee, situated around a wooden table onto which he'd set out a full tea set. I ignored the scuff marks on the table and the worn patches on the settee, and noted the binder of papers he had sitting next to him.

"I appreciate you coming out here so quickly." Ron poured our tea and settled into his seat. "You must be so busy."

"Well, family is important, and I haven't been back in years," I said, looking around the courtyard, still surprised by how empty it was.

"I'm sure you'll learn to love this place again. I've packed up your aunt's belongings—she didn't have much in her last years—and stuck everything in a storage unit. We're not in a hurry to clear it out, but you'll want to make sure you get to it before you leave Washington."

"Thanks for taking care of all that. We were so saddened to hear about what happened to Aunt Sylvia."

Calling my sister and my parents with the news had been rough. Though we hadn't kept in touch much with Aunt Sylvia since we were kids, Chrissy and I were still heartbroken by the news.

My mom had been silent on the phone, my dad doing most of the talking. I hadn't had time to drive to their home in Santa Barbara that night, so a phone call was the best I could do.

"You be careful up there, okay?" my dad said after my mom had left the call. She'd burst into tears at the news. "Are you going to bring Chrissy? I'm surprised Sylvia didn't put her in the will, too."

"I'm not really sure what that's about, but Chrissy has classes." I'd already called my sister and broken the news, and she was too focused on midterms to fly to Washington. She'd been surprised to learn that I was the only one mentioned in Sylvia's will, and I promised to find out more information.

"Yes, she was an exceptional woman." Ron nodded now. "We'd worked together for many years. I can't believe she's gone." His voice caught in his throat and he dropped his gaze to his teacup. Was it normal for a lawyer to get this upset about his client's death?

"We're so happy you're here to take over," he continued. "Of course, I don't know what your plans are exactly, but I know Sylvia would be so happy to see you breathing new life into the inn. Now, I do have a few things to go through here," he said, patting the stack of papers next to him. "An overview of the inn, its financial statements from the past few years—"

I opened my mouth to correct him—no way was I taking over the inn; I was definitely planning on selling it—but just then, a dog came running through the doors of the courtyard and launched itself at Ron, who gave a strangled squeal at the attack. I hid a smile behind my teacup as the dog, a beagle, licked all over Ron's face.

"Now you've met Lola," Ron said, pushing the dog down and wiping at his face with a handkerchief he pulled from his pocket. Lola lunged back at him, but Ron kept up his guard. Then she noticed me and turned her attention to the new body.

"Is she yours?" I asked as Lola launched herself at my side of the settee and tried to lick off my face. I rubbed her ears and held her at bay. Was she always like this when guests showed up at the inn?

"No," Ron said, folding up his handkerchief and placing it back in his pocket. "She was Sylvia's. I guess you could say she belongs to the inn now."

I stared into the pup's eyes. Ugh. She was totally pulling at my heartstrings. The new owners better be willing to adopt her, too.

"One thing I should mention." Ron's voice turned serious. "Like I said, I don't know your intentions here, but there has been one recent interested buyer. The inn has gotten offers over the years, of course, but since your aunt's health took a turn, she started looking more seriously into them."

He patted at his chest pockets, then slipped out a white business card and passed it to me.

Tony Vasco, Commercial Real Estate, it read in raised letters, a phone number etched in below the name. I looked at the other side of the card, but there weren't any more details.

Ron let out a deep sigh that almost sounded like a groan. "Mr. Vasco has been sniffing around the inn for years. He owns various B&Bs around the state and has... *plans* for the Hemlock Inn to get it in line with the decor and look of his other properties. Now, I don't want to bias you in any way," he added hurriedly, holding his hands out in front of him with a little shake. "But you should be aware of what it would mean to sell to Mr. Vasco. Of course, your aunt was seriously considering selling before her death, so maybe this is the right thing to do."

I studied the card in my hand, then looked back up at Ron. "I don't want to do anything that goes against my aunt's wishes, but I'd hate to see this place lose its character. Are there other potential buyers I could speak with?"

Ron shook his head. "Unfortunately, this is the only offer right now. Of course, I don't want to influence your opinion on this. Mr. Vasco is very good at his job and could do great things with the inn. It would probably be best if you two had a chance to speak. I can set up a meeting for the three of us this week."

I agreed, slipping Tony Vasco's card into my pocket. If this guy would pay me enough money to get my life back on track in California, I had to consider the offer. Besides, Sylvia had planned on selling to him, anyway. I should trust her judgment, shouldn't I?

"I do have one question." I turned back to Ron. "Do you have any idea why Sylvia left me the inn and not my sister?"

"You have a sister? Oh, dear." Ron looked down at the paperwork in front of him blankly, then back up at me. "I didn't realize. When Sylvia gave me your information, I thought you were an only child. That is very strange that she didn't include your sister."

Ron's phone gave a squeak, and he pulled it out of his pocket. "Oh, I need to take this," he said, reading the screen. "Do you mind if I leave you two alone for a moment?"

I nodded as Lola curled up in my lap and settled in for a nap. It didn't look like I was going anywhere anytime soon.

How odd that Sylvia would leave only me the inn. Was there a specific reason why she hadn't included Chrissy? That was something for me to figure out while I was here.

The courtyard was silent after Ron left. Blooming flowers scented the air and a fountain gurgled in the corner. I wanted to get a closer look, but Lola was too content to disturb. I leaned back against the settee and listened to her snores, letting the gurgling of the fountain wash over me.

A voice rang out loudly through the courtyard, and my head shot up. "I told you, it's the trip of a lifetime and perfectly safe!"

Another voice followed the first. "And I told you, I don't think it's a good idea!"

A couple had entered the courtyard and were bickering, so much so they hadn't noticed I was in here yet. They looked to be in their seventies, he with a shock of white hair sprouting from the top of his head, and her with a thick braid of white hair hanging down her back.

"You always make these big grand plans and expect me to come along with no complaints. I did not think this was a good idea," the man said.

The woman scoffed and rolled her eyes. "You're just getting old and can't remember anything we agree on anymore."

I could hear the laughter coming through her voice, and I had a feeling these two enjoyed the chance to bicker. They also still hadn't noticed I was sitting here. I didn't want them to think I was spying on them, so I cleared my throat, catching their attention, and gave a tiny wave when they looked in my direction.

"Sorry," I said, calling to them across the courtyard. "Didn't mean to interrupt. I didn't think anyone was here."

The man looked back to the courtyard entrance while the woman's eyes landed on me and she took a few steps closer, a warm smile spreading across her lined cheeks.

"Miles, it looks like we have a visitor," she said, turning her head towards the man. "Did you know someone was coming in today?"

The man grunted and began patting his chest, reaching into his jacket pocket and pulling out a pair of glasses. He slipped them on and turned his gaze fully on me. His eyes were clear and intense. I felt like I was looking into the face of an owl.

"I'm Simone Evans," I said, standing up and pushing Lola off my lap. She grumbled and curled up on the settee instead.

"How lovely to meet you, Simone." The woman shook my outstretched hand. Her hand was soft, her grip secure, and I found myself missing the pressure as she let go. "I'm Estelle Adler, and this is Miles." She waved behind her to the man who had now joined us.

They were the same height and had matching lines around their eyes, which deepened when they smiled. This was obviously a couple who, though they bickered with words, had spent many years happy.

"Don't mind our little argument," she added, smiling at her husband. "Someone has forgotten they agreed to take their wife skydiving." Miles grunted and rolled his eyes.

Skydiving? Who had I come upon at Aunt Sylvia's inn, the Knievels? "Are you two guests of the inn?" I realized I'd been staring at them and hadn't said a word while I tried to reconcile the image of skydiving with the two people in front of me.

Estelle's smile deepened. "Not quite," she said, her eyes flicking to Miles. "We come for the pastries at the bistro here."

"There's a bistro here?" I asked. There hadn't been a bistro when I visited as a kid, but, as I was learning, that was a long time ago, and a lot had changed.

Estelle nodded, and Miles cocked his head at me. "Are you staying here? Tracy didn't mention any new guests today."

"Who's Tracy?" I asked.

"Ah, Miles, Estelle, how lovely to see you both!" Ron said as he entered the courtyard.

The couple in front of me turned at the sound of the lawyer's voice and greeted him like an old friend. I had a feeling he was, that there was a history at this inn I was only beginning to discover.

"I see you've met Ms. Evans," Ron said, turning towards me and brushing his hand against my elbow, guiding me into their little group.

"We have." Estelle nodded, her eyes full of laughter and

warmth. "We were just saying we didn't realize anyone was arriving today, and I think we scared the poor girl."

I started to correct her, as they hadn't scared me at all—I just wasn't used to such kindness recently, and after the big city living, it was taking a moment to get used to—but Ron swept in, chuckling and squeezing Estelle's arm like an old friend.

"Excuse my appalling manners, I should've been clearer," he said, turning his twinkling gaze onto me. Had his eyes shone so brightly when the two of us were talking? "This is Sylvia's niece, Simone. She's come to take over the Hemlock Inn."

I cringed at his choice of words. "I'm not sure what I want to do with this place," I said hurriedly into the silence that stretched out after Ron's statement. "I've never run a business before. I'd love to learn more about the inn, but I also need to be practical about my decision."

Tony Vasco's offer was more appealing than trying to run a business, so I didn't want people thinking I had other plans.

Ron paused, then cleared his throat. "Of course. As I've said, I shouldn't make assumptions about your plans. I know Sylvia thought so highly of you. I'm sure she's trusted you to make the right decision."

"Sylvia was a wonderful woman," Miles said. He put his hand on my arm, and I could detect genuine sadness in his eyes. "We were so sorry to lose her. We always figured she had more family than she was letting on. She never did share much with us about her personal life. But we're so happy to meet you! Right, Estelle?"

"Of course, dear. What a pleasant surprise," she said with a smile. "I'm guessing you'll be helping with the charity auction as well?"

I glanced over at Ron. "What charity auction?"

"Of course, there's still so much to tell you about," Ron said with a smile. "This year, Pine Brook is putting on the yearly charity auction for the Children's Art Studio in Holliston. Normally Holliston puts on the event, but this year we're in charge of it, and the event will happen here at the inn." He practically puffed up with pride at the thought of his town putting on this event.

"Well, we do apologize for the interruption," Miles said, patting his chest again and checking his pockets. Did he intentionally look like he was always searching for something? With his white hair standing on end and the elbow patches, he reminded me of a forgetful college professor. "We were just passing through to the bistro. I hear Pierre has new pastries this week."

He and Estelle said their goodbyes and walked out the other end of the courtyard, Estelle's arm looped through Miles'.

"Who were those people?" I asked, turning back to Ron once they were out of earshot.

He picked up the binder and started flipping through papers. "Oh, the Adlers? I'm sorry, Ms. Evans, I keep forgetting you're new here," he said with a laugh. "I should've explained sooner. The inn doesn't only see out-of-town visitors or tourists. With the bistro in the back, it's turned into a popular haunt for the locals as well. Estelle and Miles are here at basically every meal. They're retired, their children grown and moved away, but they are still active in town. I'm sure you'll get to know them soon."

Ron pulled out some documents for us to review and I tried to focus on the spreadsheets in front of us, but I couldn't stop thinking about this bistro and how popular it was with the town.

So, not only did I have an entire inn to deal with, but there was a bistro to manage, too? Tony Vasco's offer was looking more appealing by the minute. Why did Aunt Sylvia think I could handle all of this?

3

_____

R on took me through a few of the documents he had in hand. Numbers swam in front of my eyes. All I could think about was how much easier it would be to sell this place, instead of trying to run it myself, regardless of whether Tony Vasco was going to sanitize this place and turn it into another cookie-cutter B&B.

For now, I simply wanted to spend some time getting to know the place my aunt loved.

At one point, Ron's head perked up, and he looked towards the lobby. "I think I hear Tracy," he said, somehow picking up sound from this far away. "It's time you meet her."

"Sure," I said, surprised by his serious tone. "Who's Tracy?"

He leapt out of his seat and pulled me up next to him, leading me out of the courtyard as he spoke. "The inn's general manager. She oversees the day-to-day operations. Since Sylvia's death, she's taken over more of the running of the inn. She began working here about fifteen years ago when your aunt needed more help in the inn. I had told her you were coming by today, but I'm not sure if she remembered." His voice had taken on a strain that hadn't been there before.

A woman was standing at the front desk as we walked up, and I took this to be Tracy from the way Ron stood up straighter. She was tall and broad, with black dreadlocks running down her back, held back in a ponytail, and a nose ring poking out from her dark brown skin. Tracy looked to be in her early forties, and I wondered what she'd been like when she'd shown up in her twenties.

"Tracy, there you are, my dear," Ron said, approaching the front desk, his arm looped through mine.

Tracy had the phone pressed against her ear, and she flicked her eyes up to me, taking me in in one glance and tossing me aside as she turned back to the phone. A chill went through me at her look.

Ron shot his eyes over to me and gave a tiny smile when I caught his eye. He leaned across the desk, closer to Tracy, as if trying to have a private conversation with her, even though the lobby was empty and I could hear every word.

"This is Sylvia's niece," he whispered, turning his back so I couldn't quite see what they were saying. Tracy looked up at me, skimming me from head to toe, and rolled her eyes as she turned back to the phone.

Ron shot me another tepid smile, and I wondered what this woman's deal was. You'd think she'd be more excited to meet the new owner of the inn.

Tracy made us wait while she finished up the call, which seemed to be about ordering more linens for the rooms and then another five minutes of catching up on the local gossip in town. I learned that Madeline's daughter finally had her baby, and Henry and Lisa's son was back in jail. I tried not to roll my eyes. Was this woman for real, or was she dragging it out simply for my benefit?

"So, I guess you're here to sell the inn." Tracy crossed her arms.

I jumped, not realizing that Tracy had finished her call. Ron reddened and opened his mouth to respond, but I just smiled.

"I'm not here to do much of anything," I said. "I just learned my aunt died. I'd like to get to know the place she devoted her life to and see where that leads me."

Tracy didn't need to know how eager I was to learn more about Tony Vasco's offer to buy, especially not while she was staring daggers at me. What was her problem? You'd think she'd want to get to know Sylvia's niece, but her energy the whole time I'd been over here was antagonistic.

"Don't worry." Ron patted Tracy's hand. "We won't do anything without informing you first. I know how important this place is to you; I want to make sure you feel good about the decision too."

Given the way she'd treated me just now, would Tracy agree to do whatever I decided? Or would she get in the way of selling the inn?

"Oh dear," Ron said, checking the time on his watch against the grandfather clock standing against the far wall. "I forgot I needed to check in with a client back at the office. It won't take long, so why don't you stay here?" he asked, gesturing to the back of the front desk where Tracy was standing. "You two can chat more about the inn and your aunt, and I'll be right back." He didn't give me a chance to respond before scurrying off to his office.

I smiled up at Tracy, who ignored me and turned her attention to the guest who had gotten in line behind me.

Shrugging, I went to join her on the other side of the desk, unsure of what else to do but follow Ron's guidance.

Tracy was efficient, that's for sure. She got the couple standing in line checked in and laughing in no time. I found myself grinning along as she joked around with the guests and passed them the key to their room. Where had she been hiding this personality?

"Sounds like you have a good rapport with these guests," I said, once the couple had headed up the stairs to their room.

"You have to, to be good at this job," she said, throwing me a glance over her shoulder. "So what do you do?"

"I work in mixology." She didn't need to know I'd just been fired for assaulting a customer.

Tracy snorted. "So you're a bartender? Why do you want to run an old inn? I'm sure you have much better things to be doing with your time than roughing it in the mountains of Washington."

I shrugged. "No one knows how to deal with people like a bartender, right? Like I said, I'm interested in learning more about my aunt and this inn. I used to come here when I was a kid with my sister. That was years ago, though."

I glanced around again, still shocked that this was the place Chrissy and I had spent so many summers together, playing in the garden, spying on guests who looked so fancy with their long coats and scarves, and playing tag in the hallways. It looked the same, and also different, and I wondered if that sensation would go away. Well, even if it didn't, I didn't plan on staying around long, so it didn't matter.

Suddenly, Tracy was right in front of me, her hands on her hips as she loomed over me by several inches, and I tried not to shrink away. "Look, I don't know what you're telling Ron, but I know what you plan to do with this inn."

Before I could respond, she bulldozed over me.

"Save it," she went on. "I know your type. You just want to get rid of this old place and pick up a pretty penny. Well, don't forget you're now dealing with people's livelihoods here. Don't screw it up."

My mouth fell open as I tried to think of a response, but she'd seen right through me. I was planning on doing exactly what she said.

Why did I care what she thought, though? Yes, she'd probably worked closely with my aunt over the years, but that didn't mean we needed to be friends. I'd rather unload her off to Tony Vasco and make him deal with her.

"Look, I'm not here to mess with anyone's job," I said as Tracy turned back to the front desk. "And I don't mean to step on your toes. I don't know why you're putting up such a fight already, but I promise I'll do my best with the inn." Sylvia probably wouldn't want me getting into a tussle with her general manager, so I left it at that.

Tracy didn't respond to my announcement, so I shrugged and pushed off from the counter. I'd had enough of this woman's toxic mojo and decided to look around instead.

It was crazy to even think about running a business like this. I had no clue how to do it, and I would probably make it fail. I'd already messed up two jobs in the past year; I couldn't be responsible for an entire business. Selling to Tony Vasco was the right decision, no matter what Tracy thought.

∽

I COUNTED fifteen rooms on my walk around the inn, plus the room that I was staying in. According to Ron, Aunt Sylvia lived onsite, on the first floor, in a larger suite than the rest of the rooms.

The scent of her perfume still lingered in the room. Fresh linens were on the bed, but traces of Sylvia were still all around. A wave of emotion came over me as I was transported back in time, remembering sitting with my aunt and watching her brew tea. She hadn't lived onsite back then; she and Uncle Tim had had a house in town. But this room felt like she'd lived in it forever.

The room was nicely furnished and cozy. A double bed with a quilted bedspread, a chest of drawers and a vanity made from the same dark wood as the rest of the inn, with a small bathroom attached to the room. The wallpaper was a floral print that matched the bedspread, and the floral curtains completed the theme. The curtains were pulled open, and the window looked out onto the back garden, where birds were chirping. There was a small kitchen in the back and a sitting area in the front.

Lola followed me into the room and settled herself on a dog bed next to the bed. It was a nice enough room, but I didn't know if I wanted to stay in it for more than a couple of days. It felt like Sylvia was just around the corner, waiting to tell me a joke or ask how my day was.

I left my bags in the room and headed to the bistro, led by my rumbling stomach and the smell of strong coffee. The dark wood continued in this room, with tables scattered throughout the wide area and a set of double doors that undoubtedly led to the kitchen.

"Just one today?" the man at the door to the bistro asked, walking over to me. His face lit up as he got closer. "Simone Evans! How great to finally meet you!"

He held out his hand and smiled wide. I shook it, unsure of what to think of his enthusiasm. His black hair was spiked, the tips dyed blue, and he was wearing an oversized, black-and-white striped sweater, his nails painted dark blue.

"I'm Eddy," he said, guiding me to a table by the window. "I help out at the front of the shop." He pointed to a red-haired woman in the dining room, who was taking an order from another table. "That's Penny. She's also stationed out here, and we check tables out once they're done eating. We're so happy you're in town. Have you met everyone back here yet?"

I shook my head, taking a seat and accepting the menu he slid my way. "I'm still trying to get a handle on everything," I said, flipping the menu open and glancing over the options.

"Well, there's not a lot of us, so don't worry about that," Eddy said with a smile. "You'll meet Pierre in the kitchen. He does all the cooking, and Javier helps him with the side orders and getting everything plated. And Hank manages the dishes." Eddy gestured to another man, who was carrying a stack of plates and cups away from a table. He stumbled on a woman's purse sitting on the floor, and I cringed as he almost dropped everything.

"Don't worry about him," Eddy said, moving so he was blocking my view of Hank. "He rarely drops things. So, what can I get you?"

"Just a coffee, and whatever pastry is best," I said, folding up the menu and passing it back to him.

"Coming right up."

I looked around the rest of the bistro as he left, taking in every detail. The dining area wasn't very large, but most of the tables were full. I spotted Estelle and Miles sitting at another table and gave a tiny wave when Estelle noticed me.

The red-haired woman, Penny, swung by a few minutes later with my coffee and a croissant. She placed both down in front of me and smiled.

"We're so happy you're here," she said, folding her arms across her chest. "It's great to get some fresh faces in town."

"I'm happy to be here." I took a sip of the coffee and groaned in pleasure. I was definitely going to need to keep coming back here for Pierre's coffee.

A man walked into the bistro then, carrying a large crate full of apples. He glanced around the room, then spotted Penny and walked over to us. I took another sip of my drink, watching him over the rim of the mug.

His dark hair hung long down his head, framing his face and accenting his brown eyes. His cheekbones looked like they could cut glass, but his worn jeans, grey t-shirt that had probably once been white, and loose, faded flannel told me this man didn't spend much time on catwalks. His gaze dropped to me as he approached the table and I felt my insides flip as we made eye contact.

"Nick, I thought you already dropped off the delivery for the day," Penny said, interrupting my journey into this man's eyes. His cheeks reddened as he looked away from me and I focused on my mug, trying to ignore the party happening in my stomach. Since when did I get butterflies?

"I found a box in the truck that I forgot to add to the order," Nick said. "I figured I'd bring it back now, so Pierre is all set for breakfast tomorrow. I'll go drop it off with him." He nodded to Penny and sent a grin my way.

Clearing my throat, I turned to Penny, hoping she couldn't hear the butterflies ravaging my stomach right now. "Who was that?"

"Oh, him? That's Nick, our produce supplier. Sorry, I should've introduced the two of you. I'm sure you'll get to know him very well over the next few weeks."

My eyebrows raised as I looked back in Nick's direction. Since when were produce guys so attractive? Antonio's bar had had a produce guy, but he was sleazy and always smelled like spoiled peaches.

"Well, Eddy said he already told you all about us, so I'll let you enjoy your breakfast. Let me know if I can get you anything else," she added with a wink, then walked away.

The croissant melted in my mouth at the first bite. It paired perfectly with the steaming coffee. I could get used to this kind of food. I put Nick's face right out of my mind.

Though I was enjoying my food and the atmosphere of the bistro, I was still stinging from the harshness of Tracy's words. True, she'd seen right through me and was just calling me out on something I was planning on doing, but I'd hoped to keep my plans under wraps until I'd gotten a better sense of the situation.

I wasn't interested in going right back to LA and figured I could get a couple days out of this visit before I needed to decide anything. But if Tracy was going to put up a fight the whole time, that would make this trip much harder. I stared down at the croissant, wondering what I had gotten myself into.

4

I finished the croissant and stared around the rest of the bistro, unsure of what to do with myself now.

I'd received a call from Ron a few moments ago. We made plans to meet up again the next morning, in Aunt Sylvia's office, to go over paperwork for the inn. He wanted to give me a better understanding of the inn's financials. The idea of looking at spreadsheets all morning didn't bring me much joy, but I didn't really have a choice.

At least now, I had some time to myself. I headed back to Aunt Sylvia's room to settle in.

I unpacked a few things from my bag, putting my toiletries away in the bathroom and hanging up a few dresses, shirts, and pants I'd brought with me. I hadn't known what to expect, so I'd packed for a range of activities. But not quite the weather.

Out the window, clouds gathered in the distance, hinting at rain. I hadn't been back to Washington in so long, I'd forgotten to pack for the weather. Hopefully, I'd find time to stop at a store and pick up a few things.

As I unpacked, my thoughts drifted to Tracy. Would Tony Vasco put up with her snark, or would he fire her on day one? I didn't want anyone to lose their jobs, but I couldn't help it if Tracy acted like this with everyone. Was there any chance her defensive manner would make it harder to sell the inn?

How had Aunt Sylvia worked with her? Tracy seemed like such a tiresome woman, and my aunt had been so kind. Though she had had an acerbic sense of humor, so maybe they'd bonded over that?

Whether I liked it or not, as the general manager, Tracy knew how to run this place. We were going to have to work together until I could find someone to buy the inn, then she wouldn't be my problem anymore.

I washed my face in the tiny bathroom—air travel always dried out my skin—and considered what to do next. I wasn't interested in spending any more time with Tracy, but I didn't know anyone else in town besides those people I'd met at the bistro.

Instead, I went to Sylvia's office. Ron had pointed it out to me when he was giving me the tour of the inn, though we hadn't had time to stop by the office. I'd vaguely remembered its location from when I was a kid, but Chrissy and I hadn't spent much time in Sylvia's office when we visited, so I appreciated that Ron was pointing out all these places to me.

I didn't pass anyone as I left my room and headed back downstairs. Sylvia's office was in the back of the building, a few doors down from the bistro and kitchen.

The smell of her perfume hit me as soon as I opened the door. It had been a few weeks since she'd last been in here, but the scent hadn't gone away. Tears pricked at my eyes as I surveyed the room, emotion pouring over me, taking deep breaths as the memory of her fought to overpower me.

It was a small office. A desk and a chair, bookshelves on opposite walls, filled with books, and a large window running the length of the far wall behind her desk. A filing cabinet stood to the right of the desk. Her desktop computer was still on the desk, and I wondered what Ron was planning on doing with it.

Although, I suppose it was now my responsibility to figure out what to do with everything in here, right?

Trying to keep my tears at bay, I stepped over to one of the bookshelves. I gasped at the sight of a glass jar with multi-colored stones inside. Sylvia loved the beach and would gather the stones she thought were the most unique to bring home with her. A tear rolled down my cheek as I spotted another glass jar nestled onto another shelf. I'd forgotten all about this hobby of hers.

I ran my fingers along the spines of the books on the shelf. Sylvia had always loved to read, had described it as a journey into another world. My fingers settled on the spine of *The Giving Tree*, which we'd read together when I was a child. She'd kept it, after all these years? The tears were pouring down my face now.

Suddenly, loud voices carried into the office from the lobby. Were people fighting in the inn? Wiping at my tears with my hands and leaving the office, I went to investigate.

Tracy stood behind the front desk, her arms crossed and her face twisted in a scowl. A short blonde woman leaned over the counter until her face was only inches from Tracy's.

"I told you I wanted an ice sculpture in the main room." Her raised voice made a cowering Lola whimper from behind the front desk. "We need something to class things up around here." With her head tilted back, she gave the lobby a scrutinizing glance.

"Why did you tell the sculpture artist he couldn't take measurements?" she asked Tracy, narrowing her eyes. "I'm getting that sculpture. The auction is in less than two weeks and you can't go around making changes like this."

Tracy rolled her eyes. "Listen, Bethany, I don't know how many times I need to tell you this, but you don't get to dictate how this place looks because you're co-chair," Tracy said, not backing down from the woman's glare. "I'm in charge of the inn, and I'm telling you we aren't putting up an ice sculpture."

"Just because Sylvia croaked, doesn't mean you're in charge. I'm co-chair and what I say goes!"

A spark ignited in Tracy's narrowed eyes. "How dare—"

I hurried between them, putting my arms out like stop signs. "Why don't we all take a breath?"

Both women looked up at me, Bethany's gaze dismissive, Tracy's face unreadable.

"Excuse me? We're talking here," Bethany said, gesturing between herself and Tracy. "Who are you?"

I opened my mouth to respond, but Tracy beat me to it. "This is Simone. She's running the inn now," she said with a hint of bitterness.

A smile broke across Bethany's face and she took a step closer to me. "Sylvia's niece, of course! How lovely to meet you." She shot a sneer in Tracy's direction. "I'm trying to do my job here, but someone is standing in my way. Can you please do something with her?"

Tracy scoffed and Bethany smirked. This was what I got for trying to be helpful. After losing the temp job because of the chickens and getting fired from Antonio's bar after standing up to that drunken jerk, you'd think I'd learned my lesson and stop this tendency of getting involved in other people's fights.

"Listen, why don't we just take a break?" I turned to Bethany. "There are some nice pastries in the bistro. Have one on me, and then we can discuss this ice sculpture." I smiled, hoping the customer service skills I'd picked up at Antonio's bar had carried over into this new life.

In an instant, Bethany's smile turned into a scowl. Guess those customer service skills weren't transferring. "I'm not interested in sitting around and snacking on Pierre's weird experiments. I'm trying to raise money for this stupid town. Once you've realized who's in charge here, you know where to find me."

With that, she turned on her heel and stormed out of the inn, her long blonde hair flapping down her back. Lola took a few steps out from behind the desk and sniffed in the direction of the departing woman, then settled back down on her dog bed, looking pleased that the argument was over.

"How weird was that?" I asked Tracy, gesturing over my shoulder. "Who was that woman?"

"I can handle myself," Tracy said, her voice devoid of emotion. "I don't need you riding in here and trying to save me from anything. This inn doesn't need you, either. Bethany is a pain, but if you want to take over this place, you're going to have to get used to it."

"I-I'm sorry," I said, my eyes widening. "I didn't mean to get in the middle of anything—"

"Well, you did," Tracy said, turning to the computer on the desk. "I don't need someone coming in and saving me. I've got some accounting to take care of, so why don't you leave?"

So much for getting her to open up to me. What was her problem? She typed away at the computer for a moment, her face determined, then turned away from the front desk, her back to me. I knew when I wasn't wanted.

With nothing else to do and night coming soon, I headed back to my room, preparing for an early night in. I would leave Tracy and her attitude to deal with until tomorrow.

5

———

I woke up the next morning and stared at the ceiling for a heartbeat, struggling to remember where I was. The events of the past couple of days rushed over me and I shut my eyes as I thought about my new responsibility.

After yesterday, and the less-than-warm welcome from Tracy, I wasn't exactly regretting my decision to come to Pine Brook, but I was beginning to worry that I had bit off more than I could chew.

The front lobby was quiet as I descended the stairs, and I didn't run into any other guests as I left my room. Ron had mentioned this was a quieter time at the inn, though things were supposed to pick up with the charity auction later this month.

Tracy was at the front desk, as I expected. She was staring at the computer, her fingers flying across the keyboard. Did she have a pen pal she was emailing? Or was she cataloguing all my failures into a burn book?

It didn't matter what she thought about me; I was here to sell an inn, and nothing was going to keep me from that goal. I strode over to the front desk, my defenses up in case she wanted another fight.

"Good morning." I rested my arms on the front desk.

Tracy glanced up and sneered. "Still here?" she asked, picking up her typing again. "I would've thought the inn was too much to handle, and you'd gone home."

I rolled my eyes. Was she trying to make me hate her, or was she like this with everyone?

"I can't exactly leave until we settle things with the inn. I'm meeting Ron to go over some paperwork."

Tracy glanced up, an icy smile on her face. "There's a line behind you." She leaned around me and greeted the person who had gotten in line while I was talking. I stepped to the side, trying unsuccessfully not to let the annoyance show on my face.

Fine; if she didn't want to talk, we didn't have to talk. My meeting with Ron wasn't for another twenty minutes, but I wasn't interested in standing around and waiting for Tracy to berate me again. She didn't have to like me, but I also didn't have to put up with her attitude.

The halls of the inn were quiet as I headed towards Aunt Sylvia's office, where I was meeting Ron. We had a lot to go over, and I needed to focus. I pushed open the door to Sylvia's office, hoping he would be here soon.

My stomach jumped at the sight of someone sitting in Sylvia's office chair. I immediately recognized Bethany's long blonde hair.

"Oh, you scared me!" I put my hand over my racing heart and took a step into the room. What was she doing here?

It took my brain a moment to catch up to what my eyes were seeing.

Her face was drained of color.

Her eyes were staring, unseeing, up towards the ceiling.

And a silver-plated letter opener stuck out from the center of her chest.

This was Bethany.

AN HOUR LATER, I was sitting in the courtyard, a blanket wrapped around my shoulders, clutching a mug of hot tea in my hands. Though the tea was warm, I couldn't stop the feeling of cold in my chest.

A body. I'd just been in the same room as a dead body. This was a new one for me.

I came to the Hemlock Inn for a trip down memory lane and a break from my real life. I hadn't signed up for a starring role in the opening scene to an episode of Law & Order! I wasn't built for finding dead bodies. My heart was still pounding in my chest from the shock.

I flicked my gaze to the other side of the courtyard where Tracy was speaking with a police officer, who was taking notes. I knew I was next. I'd seen enough crime shows to understand how questioning a witness works, but I never thought I'd be a witness that someone would need to question.

I looked down at my hands, surprised to find them empty before realizing that I'd set the teacup down on the table next to me. Were blackouts part of the trauma of discovering a dead body? They didn't show that on the crime shows.

What was Tracy saying to the police officer? She'd come running in when she'd heard my scream, and she'd guided me out when it was clear I couldn't move. She'd sat me down in the courtyard, gently, and I had a fleeting thought about where this gentle person had been when she was sneering at me earlier. Then I remembered Bethany's dead body was in the other room, and I stopped thinking about how Tracy was treating me.

When I'd come out of Sylvia's office, Pierre and Javier from the bistro, and a couple guests who had checked in just that morning, had been gathered in the lobby.

Miles was there, cradling a handkerchief and glancing around with wide eyes, while Estelle was standing next to him, completely still. We made eye contact, and I noticed an odd gleam in her eyes that hadn't been there before, as if she was almost thrilled by what was happening.

I turned back to my mug of tea, which was back in my hands. Bethany's vacant, dead eyes flashed through my mind. Who would do this? Who would kill Bethany? She'd been so mean to Tracy yesterday, and to me. Now she was dead. In my aunt's office! Well, I guess it was now my office until I sold the inn.

Did Tracy know what happened to Bethany? She had been annoyed with Bethany the day before, though I didn't think her feelings would've led to murder. It was probably hard to work in a customer-facing job like this, where you had to help people with a smile, regardless of what they did.

Of course, Tracy hadn't exactly had a smile on her face yesterday when she'd told Bethany to leave. And I knew as well as anyone the anger a customer like Bethany could elicit. My knuckles were still sore from my altercation at Antonio's bar.

I glanced back up to where Tracy was talking to the police officer. Was she telling them about yesterday? Did she kill Bethany?

I glanced at my watch. Where was Ron? He was officially

late for our meeting. Had something happened to him? Did he know what happened here?

A tall blonde woman entered the courtyard, wearing a long white coat, like a doctor. She spoke briefly with the officer who was talking with Tracy, then turned and went back into the inn. Who was that? Some kind of forensics specialist or coroner?

Suddenly, a police officer was standing in front of me. Over his shoulder, Tracy and the first officer were both staring at me.

"I've got a few questions, if you don't mind," the officer in front of me said, then took a seat across from me. I kept my eyes on him and gulped.

What had I gotten myself into? Being questioned by police was not what I had signed up for.

6

Officer Scott introduced himself and began flipping through his notepad, looking for a clean sheet of paper. If I could hazard a guess, he was in his early twenties, with a patch of hair on his chin. The faint hair on his cheeks probably indicated he could only grow out that tiny patch on his chin. His uniform was baggy on his gangly frame, and he stood several inches taller than me. How long had he been a police officer? He looked barely out of high school.

Officer Scott flipped through the pages of his notepad again, his hands shaking and beads of sweat gathering above his lip, where his facial hair didn't reach. He looked up at me then, having found a blank page, and I smiled, hoping he hadn't noticed me staring. I tried to ignore the beads of sweat and focused on his words.

Curiosity got the better of me. "Who was that woman?" I asked. "Who came into the courtyard just a moment ago? The blonde?"

"Oh, that's Dr. Haynes, the medical examiner from Seattle. She works for the county and goes out to all the crime scenes in the area," he explained.

Ah, that made sense. Pine Brook was too small to have its own medical examiner, so of course they'd work with someone through the county. That happened on TV shows sometimes, right?

"Could you please walk me through the events from this morning?" Officer Scott asked, his professionalism not hiding the tremor in his throat. Poor guy was nervous. Was this his first time questioning a witness?

I took him through my morning, explaining how I was planning on meeting Ron in Aunt Sylvia's office, and instead ended up finding a dead body. I shuddered, remembering Bethany's dead eyes and bloody chest. I was going to have a hard time sleeping tonight.

"And you inherited this inn?" he asked, flipping to a different page in his notepad and reading something he'd written earlier.

I nodded. "Ron called me a couple days ago, telling me about my aunt's death and the inn." Had it really only been two days since I'd gotten that call? It felt like a lifetime ago now. "I came up as soon as I could."

"Did you know the victim? Bethany Stevens?"

I shook my head. "No, I met her yesterday for the first time. Well, we didn't exactly meet. She was arguing with Tracy about the charity auction. I tried to calm Bethany down, but she left in a huff. I went to bed early after she left, so I could be prepared for my meeting with Ron this morning." Who still hadn't shown up. Was everything okay with him? I hadn't known him long, but he didn't seem like the type of person to miss meetings.

Officer Scott nodded and scribbled in his notepad. How

legible were his notes going to be today? Was this guy actually going to find Bethany's killer?

I realized then that what I was seeing wasn't nerves, or not just nerves. What he saw today had freaked him out. I thought then about whether this town had very many murders. Probably not.

A town of twenty thousand people wasn't likely to attract much violent crime, even if it was a tourist destination. Officer Scott probably thought it would be cool to wear a gun and a badge, and now he faced a murder. It was a lot to take in.

And now I was going to have to sell the inn after a murder had occurred here. Why did I even agree to come to Washington?

Officer Scott cleared his throat. "Can I please see your hands? We need to check for any blood or other evidence," he explained at my questioning gaze.

I held my hands out in front of me, ignoring the unsettling way he examined them, instead staring at the cowlick I could see at the back of his head as he leaned over. My hands were clean—I hadn't gotten anywhere near Bethany —but I understood why he needed to look. He added some notes to his notepad.

Officer Scott had a few more questions for me, which we went through quickly. I was tempted to ask him if he had many suspects. This was a small town, so I guessed that made it easier to figure out who was involved.

I hadn't had a great first impression of Bethany when I'd met her the day before, and it probably wouldn't be all that hard to find anyone else who'd had issues with her. How close was Officer Scott to figuring this all out?

My thoughts drifted to Tracy. Though they'd been upset with each other, their fight yesterday had felt more like

Tracy was used to this kind of behavior from Bethany and put up with it.

Did other residents in town feel the same way? Clearly someone decided they'd had enough of her. Officer Scott might have a tough job in front of him if everyone hated Bethany.

"Ms. Evans?"

I looked up then, realizing that Officer Scott was still talking, and I'd missed one of his questions. "Sorry," I said, giving my head a shake to clear my thoughts. "Got distracted. What did you say?"

"I need you to confirm your address and phone number," he said, holding out his notepad. I took it and scribbled down my details, hoping this was the end of our conversation.

My mind also flitted to the idea of flipping through his notes, to see what he'd learned today. Even though I wanted to get out of here as soon as I could and forget all about Bethany and this inn, I was still a little curious about what had happened. Would he notice if I took a peek?

Officer Scott cleared his throat and held out his hand, clearly thinking I was taking too long with his notepad. These were probably private notes that only the police should see. I smiled tightly and passed the notepad back to him, hoping he hadn't realized what I was considering doing.

"Thank you," he said, glancing over the information I'd written. "This is all very helpful."

"Of course," I said, standing and making my way to the front of the courtyard. "I want to help in any way I can. I put down my personal cell phone number, so don't hesitate to call if you have any more questions. I'll be in California, but I can talk whenever you need me."

Though I wanted to get to know the Hemlock Inn as an adult, a dead body was too much to handle. Ron and I would have to email to figure out how to sell this place.

Officer Scott shook his head and my heart sank. "I'm sorry, Ms. Evans, but we need you to stay in town. The detective that's leading this investigation is out on assignment right now, and she's going to want to talk to you again."

"You can't be serious," I said. "I gave you all the information I have." What more did they want from me? I was not interested in hanging around after finding a dead body. I still got chills thinking about Bethany's eyes staring up at me.

"I'm sorry, miss," he said earnestly. "You can't leave yet."

"Am I even safe here? There's a murderer running around!" A hint of hysteria crept into my voice.

"I'm sorry, I'm just doing my job," he said with a grimace.

Well, this was perfect. Officer Scott left me then, promising to stay in touch if anything changed. The last thing I wanted to do was stay in this town and wait around for some detective to question me.

Of course, I couldn't exactly go back home, either, given that eviction notice. I'd been counting on the money from selling the inn to get my life back on track. Had Sylvia known what she was doing by throwing me a lifeline in the form of the inn when my ship was sinking? I'd bet she didn't expect a dead body to show up!

I went into the bistro, looking for another cup of coffee. Heads swiveled in my direction. Clearly people knew about Bethany's death. I nodded a greeting to Eddy as I entered and took a seat at the table I'd had the day before. I tried to ignore the silence that blanketed the bistro as I settled in.

"Hey doll, how are you doing?" Eddy asked, coming over to my table.

I shrugged. "About as well as you'd expect. Can I get a cup of coffee? I feel like I'm about to conk out from exhaustion." Chrissy always said I needed to cut back, that my three daily cups would give me a heart attack before I was forty, but I couldn't seem to quit the stuff.

"Of course," Eddy said with a smile, squeezing my shoulder. He came back a few minutes later with my coffee and dropped a plate with a brownie next to it.

"Shh," he said with a wink. "Don't tell anyone."

I smiled and took a big bite, savoring the chocolate. "You're a lifesaver, Eddy."

"It's my job," he said, his grin widening. "I saw you talking to the police. Do they know what happened?"

I shook my head and swallowed the brownie. "Nothing they're telling me. I don't even know what happened. Did you know Bethany?"

"Everyone in town knew Bethany. It was kind of hard not to."

"What do you mean?"

Eddy sighed and glanced around, as if looking to see if anyone was listening. My eyebrows rose at his action, but I didn't say anything.

"Bethany made herself known in town, even if not everyone liked what she did. I know it's not right to speak ill of the dead, but honestly? I'm not surprised she's dead."

My eyebrows shot up even higher, but before I could ask more questions, Ron popped his head into the bistro, his eyes flitting around the space. He spotted me and hurried over, his cheeks red from the cold or exertion, I couldn't quite tell.

"Simone, there you are," he said, putting his hand on my arm. "We need to talk."

What now?

7

I followed Ron to his office in town in my rental car. He was located on Main Street, and it seemed like most of the businesses were on this street as well.

We met outside a beige-colored building attached to a small sandwich shop, with an alley on the other side. Ron led me through the reception area of the office, nodding to a woman seated behind the receptionist's desk. She had striking red hair that sprang out from her head in tiny curls. I shot her a smile as we passed.

"Oh, you must be Simone!" she said, hopping up out of her seat. "Can I just say how sad I was to hear about what happened with your aunt? It's such a tragedy, but we're so happy you're here!"

"Theresa, not now," Ron said, giving his head a sharp shake. Theresa's smile fell, and she looked between the two of us, trying to read the situation. I sent her a small smile and followed Ron further back into the building.

It was a one-story building, with a door leading to the private offices. We walked down a short hallway with three doors down either side. These must have been the other lawyers who worked with Ron. All the doors were shut, except for one at the end of the hall. This was the room Ron led me to.

"I'm sorry for pulling you out of there so suddenly," Ron said as we walked down the hallway. "I got a call this morning, and, well, I wanted to get to you as soon as possible."

I opened my mouth to ask what the call had been about when Ron stopped in front of the open door at the end of the hall and gestured for me to go inside.

The office was small and cramped. Three windows were set into the far wall, though someone had drawn the blinds and only a bit of light seeped into the room.

A mahogany desk took up most of the space, along with a set of filing cabinets pushed up against the right wall. Seated on one of the chairs opposite the mahogany desk was a man. He stood as we approached and I quickly scanned this newcomer.

He was over six feet tall, with black hair cut short and brown skin, a combination of genetics and a tan. He was wearing a khaki-colored linen suit, well-fitted, and white leather shoes. A diamond-encrusted gold watch flashed from his wrist. This man clearly bathed in money. He smiled when he saw me, and a dimple broke out on one cheek.

"Simone, this is Tony Vasco," Ron said from behind me.

Ah, of course. Sylvia's potential buyer. Did it bother me that he looked like a sleazy car salesman? I pushed the thought out of my head and stepped forward, shaking the man's outstretched hand.

"It's great to meet you," I said.

His hand enveloped mine, and he pumped it vigorously. "The pleasure is all mine, Ms. Evans," he said, his voice husky and lightly accented. Brazilian? Somewhere south of the border.

"Please, call me Simone," I said, taking a seat in the other chair opposite Ron's desk.

"As long as you call me Tony. I appreciate you meeting with me," he continued, nodding to Ron, who shut the office door and took a seat behind his desk. "Ron called me as soon as he knew you were coming up, and I asked him to set up a meeting for us."

"Well, I was just thrilled to hear about your offer to buy the inn." I crossed my legs and leaned forward, eager to finally feel like I was in control of something. "I loved my aunt, and I loved visiting this place as a kid, but I'm not cut out for running a business. I understand you and Sylvia had been discussing a deal before her death? Why don't you tell me about it?"

Tony and Ron exchanged a look that I couldn't read. "Simone, I appreciate your desire to sell the inn quickly," Tony said. "Not everyone is cut out for running their own business," he added with a bark of laughter, then sobered up. "But the situation has changed. I understand you discovered that dead body at the inn?"

I nodded. News really did travel in this town. "Yes, it was definitely a shock, but I understand the police are doing what they can to solve the crime."

"Did they say anything about their investigation?" Ron asked.

"Nothing specific. I think they're keeping their options open until they learn more. Are you concerned that their investigation may disrupt business at the inn?" I turned to Tony with my question. "They said they would try to move quickly with the crime scene since it is a place of business."

"It's not that," Tony said. "Have you been involved in a murder investigation before, Simone?"

"I can't say I have," I said with a laugh, trying to keep the conversation light, then shut my mouth when I saw the look on his face. Tony Vasco had dropped his genial smile. I looked over at Ron, whose brow was furrowed.

"Well, I have," Tony said. "You don't make a name for yourself in the real estate business and not end up in the occasional murder investigation."

I opened my mouth to respond, then thought better of it and shut it. Most people didn't find themselves in the middle of a murder investigation, and this guy admitting that he'd been in more than one did raise my suspicion-meter. However, I wanted him to buy the inn; I wasn't going to call him out on anything right now.

"If guests decide they don't want to come to a crime scene, or if the police take too long in their investigation, it could seriously hurt the Hemlock Inn's finances," Ron explained to me. "I understand there have already been some cancellations. Who knows what will happen if this goes on for too long?"

"Obviously we don't know what the future holds," Tony cut in. "But I can't in good conscience initiate a purchase of the inn while there's a killer on the loose. I'd been led to believe that Pine Brook was a safe town, but at this rate..." He sat back and held out his hands in a *who knows?* gesture. "I have a certain image to uphold, and murder is not part of that image."

As he spoke, I pictured dollar signs running down a drain. "I'm sure this will pass," I said, leaning forward, my voice desperate. "Nothing has changed about the inn. It's still the same place you've been wanting to buy."

"That may be, but I can't ignore bad press. Unless this murder gets solved quickly, I can't buy the inn." With that, he stood, nodding to Ron. I watched, helpless, as he walked to the office door.

"Simone, lovely to meet you. I do wish it had been under better circumstances." He gave a tiny bow, then left the office.

The room was silent after he left, as if Tony Vasco had taken all the air out of the room with him. I turned back to Ron, my mind blank.

"I am sorry about that." Ron's face was pained. "I know you were interested in Mr. Vasco's offer. It doesn't sound like it's completely off the table. I'll give him a call in a couple of days and see if he's changed his mind. I want to make sure the Hemlock ends up in the right hands."

"Thanks," I said, my voice soft. "I think I should get going."

"Oh, I did want to apologize for missing our meeting this morning," he said. "My mother called to discuss getting brunch this weekend, and I lost track of time. I promise I'm not normally like this. I hate that you had to go through that alone."

I'd forgotten about our meeting this morning. All I could think about was the loss of Tony Vasco's offer to buy the inn and Bethany's dead eyes staring up at me. What an awful couple of days I was having!

"That reminds me," I said. "The police were asking about security cameras this morning. I take it Sylvia didn't want them installed? Am I even safe here, or are the guests safe, with a killer running loose?"

Ron's cheeks reddened at the question. "I assure you, Sylvia took security very important. Yes, there were no cameras, but guests always knew to lock the front door if they were going to be out at night. We've never had anything like this before. Something you and Tracy should consider is installing a security system. It would probably help inspire more confidence from Mr. Vasco, knowing that you were reinvesting in the inn."

How much was a security system going to cost? I wanted to keep us all safe, but all I could see was money spinning down the drain.

"By the way, here are some financials for you to look over." Ron gathered some papers on his desk and stuck them into a file folder. He passed the folder across to me. "That's our yearly profit-and-loss statement for the past five years, plus the projections for the next six months. Normally, Sylvia would run all the numbers at the inn, but she asked me to hold on to some things when she got sick. Tracy and I had a weekly meeting where we went over everything with the inn's accountant, but it's probably best if the two of you discuss the situation and think about what to do next."

I took the stack, ignoring how thick it was, and tried to forget how much I hated math class in school. I promised to stay in touch if anything came up, and he agreed to do the same.

I made my way out of his office, staring out at the world in front of me but not seeing anything. I had a file full of numbers I didn't want to deal with, an inn I might not be able to sell, and I still couldn't get Bethany's face out of my head. I found my car and went back to the inn on autopilot.

If Tony Vasco didn't want to buy the inn, could we find another buyer? I'd been assuming I'd leave Washington with my pockets full of money from the sale, but now it was looking like I might have to head back to California with my tail between my legs and Sylvia's inn in shambles because of the murder investigation. What was I going to do?

8

"You found a dead body? You've been gone for a day!"

I could picture Chrissy's expression as I described what had happened at the inn. Her brow furrowed, her eyes narrowed in confusion, probably holding the phone out in front of her and staring at it. Again wondering how her younger sister managed to get herself into another crazy situation.

Getting evicted and then fired for punching a customer all in the same day wasn't enough. I also had to find a body in our aunt's pride and joy. I shook my head to myself, also wondering how I managed to get into these kinds of situations. I wasn't doing it on purpose, I swear.

"Tell me more about the body," Chrissy said. "How long do you think it had been in the office before you found it? Did they call in a forensic pathologist? Pine Brook is a small town. They probably had to call in someone from Seattle to look at it. When do you think they'll do the autopsy?"

I rolled my eyes as Chrissy chattered on, asking more and more grotesque questions. I'd gone back to my room once I'd gotten back to the inn. Lola had followed me in and was curled up on the bed.

I'd called Chrissy, hoping she could reassure me about everything and help me see reason in everything that was going on, but I'd forgotten that she was obsessed with true crime.

She'd always read mysteries when we were kids and had gotten swept up in the rush of true crime documentaries that had come out in recent years. I was surprised she didn't offer to come down here and snoop around herself.

"I don't really have any details," I said, cutting her off. I wasn't in the mood to debate potential murder weapons with her, particularly when I'd seen the letter opener sticking out of Bethany's chest.

"A detective wants to talk to me tomorrow, do some more questioning," I continued. "I'll probably get more information then. I just want to focus on anything but this. How are things at home?"

I flipped open the file Ron had given me, took in the spreadsheets and highlights, and flipped it back shut. I'd drop it off with Tracy as soon as I was done talking to Chrissy and see if she could figure it out.

"Oh, fine," Chrissy said, her voice losing the energy it had had when she'd been discussing blood spatter patterns. My sister, the freak. "Mark's office is having a party this week to celebrate a big case they've just closed, so I'll probably go to that..."

As Chrissy chattered on about home life and her daughter, I found my thoughts returning to Bethany. Though I hadn't known the woman well or liked her much from what little I had seen of her, I still didn't think she had deserved to die.

It also seemed odd that she was killed in Aunt Sylvia's

office. What was she doing back there? The building didn't have much security, so technically, anyone could've walked into the office.

Ron had told me that the private documents were all locked up in file cabinets and Sylvia's computer was so old she figured no one would try to steal it. And in a town the size of Pine Brook, less than twenty thousand people, it was a good bet that belongings were safe.

In L.A., I never left my apartment without making sure every single possible entrance was locked up tight, but here, out in the woods, the next house several miles away, I could understand the relaxed security.

Still, that didn't mean there wasn't the occasional break-in at the inn, as Ron had told me, and he'd tried hard to convince Aunt Sylvia to add some security to the inn, particularly as it grew in popularity. They'd been arguing about it up to the day she died. I made another note to myself to talk to Tracy about installing security cameras.

Even though she could've gotten into the office, it still didn't explain what Bethany was doing up there. Was she meeting someone? Tracy hadn't said she was planning on meeting anyone today when we had talked, so I didn't think they were looking to reconcile or anything. And Ron was planning on meeting me back there, not Bethany.

Did Bethany know about our meeting? Was she planning on crashing it? That still didn't explain how her killer would've known to go back there. Was Bethany meeting someone back in Sylvia's office?

"Yoo-hoo, Simone? You there?" Chrissy asked.

My attention snapped back to the phone. "Sorry, what was that?"

She sighed on the other end. "I was asking if you know

how much longer you're going to be up there. Do you want me to fly up? I still don't understand why Sylvia left the inn just to you. Not that you don't deserve it, of course, but why aren't we splitting it?"

"I don't know. It is weird, but Sylvia was always weird. She probably knew how important your life is in L.A., while mine was barely hanging on by a thread."

"I guess. It's confusing."

I had to agree with her. I'd thought I'd figure out why Sylvia had done this while I was here, but her motives were still unclear.

"It's strange, finding a dead body, and I just want to make sure you're going to be okay. How long are you staying?"

"I'm not sure what I'm going to do. I still need to talk to those detectives tomorrow and see what they say." I stood and moved over to the window in my room, looking out onto the back garden.

I remembered how much Sylvia had loved her flowers when she was alive and, though the flowers were noticeably less vibrant given the cold weather, I could still see her out there, clipping roses and tossing them into a basket, her broad-brimmed hat slipping down her head.

"Do you want to talk to Mark? I can see if he knows any lawyers in Washington who can help. You'll probably want someone to help out with the estate."

"Not yet, I think," I told her. "Let me talk to the detective tomorrow and see how things seem. Plus, Sylvia's lawyer has been helpful. But I'll let you know if I want to talk to Mark."

"Honestly," Chrissy went on, "I don't know why you're staying. You should just leave. You don't even know these people."

"I mean, I can't leave yet. The police still need to talk to me some more. Plus, I don't know what to do with the inn. That buyer Sylvia had been working with thinks the murder is bad press for the inn. I can't leave until I figure out what to do with it."

"It sounds like more work than it's worth. Dealing with an inn? And now a murder investigation? It's not like you're known for your commitment to things. I have no clue what Aunt Sylvia was thinking when she left you that place."

Ouch. I guess it's true that sisters always know the best buttons to push.

"Jeez, Chrissy, tell me how you really feel," I said, smiling on my end, hoping to add some levity to the statement. Her words still felt like a punch in the gut.

She sighed. "I'm sorry, Simone, I didn't mean it like that. It's just... an inn is a huge commitment, and—"

"And I'm the worst at commitments?" This was so not the time to bring up my string of bad breakups.

"Now, come on, you know that's not what I was going to say. Now you're intentionally being difficult." I could hear her exasperation through the phone line.

"You're right, you're right," I said, looking back out the window. "I might be getting over my head here. Let me deal with the detectives tomorrow and figure out my next steps. I gotta go, but I'll call you again soon." I said my goodbyes and rushed her off the phone, ignoring her apologies and pleas to keep talking.

I tossed my phone onto the bed behind me and stared back out into the garden. It reminded me of the courtyard and the Adlers and all the quaintness I'd seen so far in this town. Hard to believe that there was a killer lurking around.

I shook my head to clear my thoughts and turned away from the window. I couldn't go anywhere right now, so there was no point in thinking about leaving. I clearly couldn't stop thinking about what was happening, anyway. Maybe it made sense to stick around and at least see what the detectives could find out. I'd talk to them the next day and hopefully get everything cleared up.

9

That first morning, after finding Bethany's body, I woke up early and couldn't fall back asleep. I'd been up half the night and couldn't get the look on her face out of my head. Who would do something like this?

Sighing, I rolled out of bed and changed, lacing up the running shoes I'd tossed into my suitcase at the last minute before leaving L.A. The shoes were old, but I didn't have it in me to get rid of them, and I liked to take them when I traveled in case I had a need for them.

I did a few stretches in the lobby, pulling my curls up into a bun to get them out of my face, then left the quiet inn, running along the road leading from the inn. I didn't feel like hanging around the inn, Bethany's face the only thing I could see, so I hoped a run might distract me.

There were few cars this early, and I found myself lulled into some kind of calm. I had never been much of a runner, but I'd also never seen a dead body before either. The sound of my feet against the pavement was the only sound I heard, except for the birds chirping in the trees.

The fresh air filled my lungs, and my head started to clear, returning to where I'd been before I found Bethany's body. Fog hung in the air, blocking my view but also wrapping me in a cocoon of serenity. I looped back after a couple of miles and gave a sigh of relief as I came back to the inn. Maybe runners were onto something with this activity.

I showered and changed, stepping out of the bathroom to the sound of my phone ringing. I picked up the device and saw my mom's face flash across the screen. Sighing, I answered.

"Chrissy told us what happened. Why didn't you call us?" my mom's voice chirped across the line.

"Hello to you too, Mom," I said, tossing my sweaty clothes into the hamper and squeezing my curls dry with a towel.

"Hello, dear. Now what is happening up there? Are you in trouble?"

I sighed, thinking up some excuse to tell her to calm her down when there was a tussle on the other end and my dad picked up the phone.

"Do you need a lawyer?" he asked, his voice so loud in the phone I had to hold it out away from me. He always talked on the phone like he needed to cover the distance between himself and the person on the other end of the line. "We could have Mark find someone to help you out."

"I don't think it's that bad," I said, but there was another tussle and my mom was back on the line.

"You need a lawyer? Do you want me to talk to Mark and see if he knows anyone?"

I rolled my eyes at the two of them. Phone calls with my parents tended to go like this, with them battling over who got to talk into the phone. It's like they'd never heard of speakerphone—even though Chrissy and I had shown it to them many, many times, since our eardrums could only handle so much shouting.

"I'm just trying to get a handle on everything. Sylvia had a buyer lined up before her death, but now that there's a murder investigation, he's not so sure if he wants to buy it." Tony Vasco's face the day before was still weighing heavily on my mind. What was I going to do if he wouldn't buy the inn?

"Sylvia was going to sell the inn?" My mom's voice was confused. "Who was she going to sell it to?"

"Some commercial real estate agent. I met him yesterday, and he has plans to add the Hemlock to a chain of B&Bs around the state."

"Oh, my. Sylvia was going to turn it into a chain?"

I furrowed my brow at her words. "Yes. Why? Does that surprise you?"

"Well, yes," she said slowly. "Sylvia and I, we...we hadn't talked in years, but... she was always so proud of that inn. I can't imagine her selling it like that..." Her voice trailed off. What wasn't she saying?

"Why didn't Sylvia include Chrissy in her will?" I asked. "It's weird she didn't leave it to both of us, right?"

"Well, I don't know. Sylvia was known for her odd decisions. Did she leave you a note or anything, explaining her reasons?"

"Not that I've seen, but I'll ask her lawyer about it the next time I see him. It feels like I'm taking something from Chrissy."

"Oh, I wouldn't think of it that way." Suddenly, my dad's voice was back on the line. I was getting whiplash with these two. "Sylvia probably had a reason for not including Chrissy. Maybe she was hoping you could run the inn, and she knew Chrissy was too busy with her family and job."

Maybe. My stomach twisted at the thought. Was I going against Sylvia's wishes by seriously considering the offer from Tony Vasco?

I glanced at my watch. I was going to be late to my meeting with that detective if I didn't get these two off the phone. I appreciated the call, but I figured a detective wouldn't appreciate tardiness.

"Listen, I have to go. Everything is going to be okay here. I'll let you know as soon as I know anything."

"Simone, just please be careful, okay? If I knew that you going up there would cause all this to happen, well..." My mom broke off then with a sob and I felt my chest tighten. At that moment, I wished I could be in her arms, safe in their home.

"We love you, Simone, okay?" my dad said, taking over the phone from my mom. "Please let us know what you need."

I swiped a tear from my eye as we said goodbye. When would all this be over?

I HEADED down the stairs to the lobby, then stopped off in the bistro to pick up a pastry. I brought it into the courtyard and settled on one of the outdoor settees, waiting for the detective to arrive. Lola trailed after me and took a seat at my feet.

I'd thought a lot about my conversation with Chrissy the day before. While I didn't want to believe that she was right, I had to admit that some of what she had said may have been true. I was getting caught up in something that really had nothing to do with me. Just because Aunt Sylvia had left me this place, didn't mean that I needed to concern myself with what happened in it. I was running away from my problems at home instead of dealing with the mess I had made for myself.

While I wasn't eager to return and move all my belongings back into my childhood bedroom, I was prepared to wrap up this conversation with the detective and take care of everything that I had left behind in California. I missed my parents more than I realized, and I wanted to see them again. I didn't think Antonio would take me back at the bar, but maybe I could find another temp agency.

Life was short, and I had to take responsibility eventually. I'd come to Washington hoping for a lifeline to save me from my jobless life, and I'd felt a duty to settle Sylvia's estate. But all it had led me to was a dead body.

As I sat, my phone chirped. A text message from Mark, offering to put me in contact with one of his lawyer friends. At first, I thought he was offering to set me up on another date, then I remembered the murder investigation. Oh, right.

Lola barked a greeting when a tall woman entered the courtyard and sauntered toward us. Detective Patel introduced herself with a firm handshake and a toss of her thick dark braid over her shoulder. Steely dark eyes peered out from her brown face.

She ruffled Lola's ears and launched into her questions. They were similar to what Officer Scott had asked the day before. What I'd done that morning, what time I'd gotten to Sylvia's office, if I'd seen or heard anything strange while I was there—excluding the dead body, of course.

"So you didn't know the victim at all?" Detective Patel asked. She'd taken out a notepad but hadn't opened it since I started talking. Did she think what I had to say wasn't interesting? Or did she have an excellent memory for this kind of stuff?

I shook my head. "No, I'd only met her the day before, briefly. I'd found her and Tracy arguing about something, and I'd tried to help diffuse the situation, but Bethany walked away."

"What were they arguing about?" Patel asked. I couldn't read the look in her eyes.

I thought back to two days before. "An ice sculpture. That sounds so dumb," I said with a laugh, "but I think they're planning some kind of event here, and Bethany really wanted an ice sculpture. Tracy didn't think it was a good idea. I didn't think they were going to come to blows or anything, but I felt I should step in."

"Why did you think you should step in?"

"I wanted to help," I said. "It seemed like something the owner should do." I pressed my sweaty hands against my jeans, palms down. I'd never been questioned before like this and clearly didn't enjoy it. Detective Patel was much more intimidating than nervous Officer Scott the day before.

I glanced around the courtyard, trying to calm my nerves, and spotted a ladybug climbing up the side of one of the flower pots. Weren't ladybugs a good sign?

"Do you have any idea what might've happened to her?" Patel asked, pulling me back into her questioning. "Who might've wanted to kill her? Why was she at the inn in the first place?"

"No clue," I said with a shrug. "I mean, I didn't know the woman. I've only been in town for a couple of days. I'm sure there are other people here who might have better insight into what happened. I'm just freaked out from having seen a dead body like that. My sister is normally the one into this kind of stuff; she's a little jealous, actually." I laughed, then shut my mouth as I realized how weird that made Chrissy seem. I didn't want this detective to think she was into this kind of stuff in a weird way; although, could you be into this kind of stuff in a normal way? Hard to say.

"Did you notice anything missing from Sylvia's office?"

I shook my head. "But I haven't spent much time in her office. You should probably ask Tracy or Ron that question." Was it possible Bethany had interrupted a robbery and gotten stabbed because of it?

"Anything else you can think of that might be helpful? Anything strange you've heard or people you've met?"

I thought back over the townspeople I'd met so far. While some had been odd, and some a little kooky, everyone had been kind, and I couldn't imagine anyone stabbing another person. Did that mean someone from outside of town had done this?

I shook my head no, and Patel made a note in her notepad. I guess I'd finally said something worth writing down.

"Where were you between nine and eleven P.M. last night?" she asked.

"Is that when Bethany was killed?"

Patel nodded.

"I was here. Well, not *here*, here, but in Sylvia's suite. I'd turned in early and didn't hear anything from the room. Do you think I killed her? Why would I do that? I didn't even know the woman!" I winced at the hysteria in my voice.

Patel took a moment before answering, scratching something else in her notepad. When she looked up, her eyes had softened. "At this point, everyone is a suspect. It's too early to pursue any one particular path."

If she thought everyone was a suspect, did that mean she

thought Tracy and Ron were suspects, too? What about the Adlers? What had I gotten caught up in?

"Are we even safe here with a killer running around?"

"I'd recommend everyone be cautious for the next few days, as we can't say for sure what the motive was," Patel said. "I'm guessing the office wasn't locked? Anyone could've gotten back there?"

I nodded. "How did you know that?"

"No one in this town locks anything, even when they should."

"What does this mean for the inn?" I asked, searching for some insight in her eyes. "I came here hoping to sell this place; is that even possible anymore?"

"Right now, this is a crime scene. The crime scene techs will work quickly since this is also a business and will try to clear things out by the end of the day so you can open the inn back up again. But we have to assume that anyone could've killed Bethany."

Oh jeez. Now I had to worry about a killer running loose?

Patel flipped her notepad closed and held my gaze. "Look, I understand you probably didn't realize what you were getting into when you came here. But we have to do our jobs here. I need to call the lab and see if they were able to lift any prints off the knife. We'll need you to stick around for a couple of days, as we may need you to come to the station to give a set of your fingerprints. Someone will be in touch."

She stood then, the interview clearly over, giving me a tiny smile as she did. I stood with her, my face numb, and watched her leave the inn, her braid swinging down her back.

I sat back down on the settee, only because I didn't know

what else to do. I'd have to get fingerprinted? Everyone was a suspect? Was I even safe here?

My head fell into my hands and I groaned. I should've listened to Chrissy and left as soon as I could. Lola hopped up onto the seat next to me and put her head in my lap, as if sensing that I needed some comforting right now. The police couldn't do anything about it if I was already back home in California, could they?

Instead, now I was stuck here, dealing with an inn I didn't want and a murder investigation I didn't need. It's like, no matter how hard I tried to be responsible, things always went wrong around me. I glanced at the clock in the court-yard. Seemed as good a time as any to get a drink.

10

S itting in the bistro, I sipped my cup of tea and watched the other patrons. Unfortunately, ten A.M. was a bit too early for wine here, but the tea was good. I'd also ordered a muffin and figured I could stuff my face with pastries until the police solved Bethany's murder.

I wasn't going anywhere until the police took my fingerprints, so I may as well take advantage of the tasty food Pierre could cook up.

I looked around the bistro as I sipped. Had one of these people murdered Bethany the day before? Everyone looked friendly enough, a few people catching my eye and waving, but what did I know about small-town drama? Maybe Bethany had finally pissed someone off too much.

"Hi, Simone, here's your muffin!" Hank, the busboy, walked over to my table from the kitchen, carrying a plate with my muffin, along with a few other items. Suddenly, he tripped over someone's bag, and everything in his hands went flying. I cringed at the sight.

"I'm so sorry," Hank said as I hurried over to help him.

Javier came out from the kitchen with a broom and dustpan. We got everything cleaned up, and I watched with sadness as the remains of my muffin were carried away. Hank promised to bring me another one, but I told him it was all right. Maybe this was a sign I didn't need a muffin.

"We know he's a mess, but you can't get rid of him," Estelle said as she and Miles approached my table.

"What do you mean?" I gestured for them to take a seat.

"Hank," Estelle clarified, a stricken look on her face. "I know he's clumsy and gets orders mixed up, but you can't fire him."

I stiffened. "I wasn't planning on firing him. I wasn't planning on firing anyone. It's not my place to decide how to run the bistro. If Aunt Sylvia and Tracy think he's good at his job, I won't mess that up."

"Good," Estelle said, sitting back with a smile.

"Hank's a good kid," Miles continued. "And he loves this town, and this inn. He just needs to work on his balance. But he'll figure it out soon, I'm sure of it."

"How long has he worked here?" I asked. Maybe he needed more time to get used to the demands of the job.

Miles and Estelle exchanged looks and were quiet for a moment. "Two years," Miles finally said, and my eyebrows shot up my forehead. Was there any hope for Hank? This seemed like the kind of job where you either picked it up or you didn't. How many more years did he need before he wasn't dropping orders?

Of course, what did I know? I'd recently been fired from a similar job for punching a customer. I wasn't exactly a role model of customer service skills.

"Enough about Hank," Estelle said. "What's going on with Bethany's murder? We saw all the police here, and it's all over town. Have they told you anything?"

I paused before responding. Detective Patel hadn't told

me I couldn't tell anyone about her investigation, but she probably wouldn't be too happy if she knew I was talking all over town about the case.

But Estelle and Miles were kind, and after my interactions with Tracy, I was looking to talk to someone who wasn't my crime-obsessed sister.

"Not much," I said after a moment. "They're looking at a few different angles. I take it this town hasn't seen anything like this before?"

Estelle and Miles shook their heads in tandem. "This is the most exciting thing that's happened in a long time," Estelle said, leaning forward.

Miles tsked at his wife. "A woman is dead, Estelle. I wouldn't call that exciting."

"You know what I mean," Estelle said with a flap of her hands. "Obviously I'm not happy about it, but it is big news." She turned back to me. "You found the body; did you see anything suspicious in the room? I heard she was stabbed. Do the police have any suspects? Do they suspect you?"

"Estelle, enough," Miles said, his voice stern. "You're scaring her." Estelle's words took a moment to register in my brain.

"Wait, suspect me? You think the police might suspect me?" I looked back and forth between the two of them, heartbeat speeding up.

Estelle and Miles exchanged another look. "Well, of course," Miles said, as if it was the most obvious thing in the world. "The person who found the body is always a suspect. Don't you watch those crime shows?"

"They give me bad dreams." I scrunched up my nose at the thought. "Do you think I should be worried about the police? Stop that," I admonished as they exchanged another look. I was getting tired of this married couple telepathy thing they had going on.

Estelle sighed and shrugged, her gaze remorseful. "The police here aren't exactly experienced at finding murderers in this town. We have more domestic disputes and drunken brawls. Nothing this serious. Did the police give any sign about any suspects?"

I shook my head, remembering my interaction with Patel. "The detective on the case didn't tell me much, but she did say that everyone was a suspect. I'm not sure what to do. I want this to get solved quickly. It can't be good for the future of the inn to have an unsolved murder." Tony Vasco was already starting to pull away; could I sell the inn while there was a murder investigation going on?

"No," Estelle said with a shake of her head, her eyes thoughtful. "I don't know how prepared the police are for something like this."

Miles sat back in his seat and began fiddling with his handkerchief. When Hank lumbered past with more orders, I considered requesting another muffin. Maybe it was best to wait until Eddy was back on duty. I could at least trust him not to drop my muffin.

"What do you two think?" I asked them after a few moments of silence. "Who do you think killed Bethany?"

They exchanged yet another glance, then both shrugged. "No idea," Miles said. "I wouldn't have said there were any killers in town before this, but clearly I was wrong. People didn't like Bethany all that much, but I don't know who'd want to kill her."

"We were out of town when it happened, shopping in the next town over," Estelle said. "So I know we're at least not suspects since there were cameras and everything to see us. But you are right that it was probably someone in town who did it. I wonder who." She looked around the bistro, as if hoping to see someone wearing an "I did it!" t-shirt.

Shopping wasn't a great alibi, but if the police did spot the Adlers on camera, then it wasn't possible for these two to have murdered Bethany. Still, could I trust them? I didn't want the inn to get shut down, and Tracy wasn't interested in talking with me about everything that was going on. Maybe these two were my only chance to figure out how to get out of this.

"You know," Estelle said, breaking into my thoughts, "the police might need some help with this. Like we said, they aren't experienced at this kind of thing, and I'm sure that detective is overwhelmed by all the work on this case."

"What are you getting at?" Miles asked, watching his wife with narrowed eyes.

"Nothing." Estelle shrugged innocently. "But I wonder if maybe they need some help. We could ask around, see what we can find out about Bethany and what she was up to the last few days of her life. And bring what we know to the police."

"Estelle, you cannot be serious," I said. "We are not detectives." That gleam in her eye that I'd noticed earlier at the crime scene was back. Someone was interested in playing detective.

"But maybe we could be," Miles said, the wheels in his head spinning. "We know everyone in town, and Simone here has a good reason for asking questions since she found Bethany's body. If we worked together, maybe we could get some clues."

"You both are crazy," I said.

But they were already planning their first steps, muttering to each other.

I shook my head. "Why would anyone tell us anything?"

"This town loves gossip," Miles said. "And they loved Sylvia. I'm sure people are lining up to talk to you about what happened."

I didn't think that was true, but as they put their heads back together and continued planning their strategy, I had to wonder: maybe this wasn't such a bad idea? I couldn't let them go snooping around where they shouldn't, but maybe if we asked some questions, we could find out some things about Bethany that the police didn't know.

And if we brought that evidence to the police, maybe they could find her killer faster. If the police found her killer faster, Tony Vasco might still be willing to buy the inn. Plus, even though Bethany had been rude, she didn't deserve to die.

"A meeting of the minds, I see," said a voice from behind us. Penny walked up and set a muffin on the table in front of me. "Sorry about Hank, Simone. Eddy's at a doctor's appointment, so we thought we'd give Hank a chance to help with the tables. Maybe not one of our best ideas."

"It's okay." I smiled. "I didn't even like that muffin all that much. This one looks much better."

"Happy to hear it," Penny said. "So what are you three talking about? Plotting some scheme?"

Miles and Estelle exchanged a glance, and guilt was written all over their faces. I hoped my face didn't look that suspicious.

"Nothing that interesting," I said with a laugh, breaking the silence. Penny didn't need to know what we were considering doing. Though, I had to wonder why she'd assumed the two of them would be involved in plotting a scheme. "Miles and Estelle are just telling me all about the town. Trying to distract me from the events of the past couple of days."

"Well, I hope they're not filling your head with tall tales," Penny said, taking Estelle's empty teacup and grinning down at the two of them. "These two are known for their troublemaking." She sent a smile my way, then left to clear another table.

"Well?" Miles implored the minute Penny was out of earshot.

"After what Penny said?" I sputtered. "You two are trying to get me into trouble!"

"We are not," Estelle said, her voice stern. "We're trying to find a killer!"

I blew out a long breath. These two were going to be more trouble than I realized. But were they right? Should we try to solve this murder? We weren't detectives, far from it, but I couldn't sit around and do nothing.

What could it hurt to ask a few questions? We'd bring anything we found out to the police, and we could stop if it got too dangerous. I had to do something to keep Tony Vasco from pulling his offer.

"While I think this is a bad idea overall, we're going to be smart and safe about this," I said finally. "We do nothing risky, and we talk to each other about what's going on."

Estelle and Miles cheered and hopped out of their chairs, ready to go grill their first suspect.

What exactly had I agreed to? And how quickly would I come to regret it?

11

I passed through the lobby, trying to think of where to go next. I wasn't a detective, that much was clear. What would Lennie Briscoe do? Probably rough up a suspect and crack a one-liner. I was all out of one-liners, but maybe I could find a suspect to talk to. But I needed to be careful—there was a killer out there, and I didn't want to get on their bad side.

I'd learned enough to know I had to proceed with caution with Tracy. With the inn's financials tucked under my arm, I practically tiptoed to the front desk. She had her back to the lobby, studying something on the ground.

I craned my neck, spotting the edge of Lola's dog bed and a flapping tail. Tracy bent over to give her a belly rub, followed by a series of kissy sounds. My gasp alerted Lola, who gave a little bark and scurried over to greet me.

Tracy stiffened like a broomstick and her usual grumpy demeanor quickly returned as she turned back to the computer.

Though I didn't want to talk to her, I had to admit that Tracy might have some valuable information since she'd been working so closely with Bethany before her death. Plus, they'd gotten into an argument the day before she was killed. That had to push her right to the top of my suspect list. Fortunately for me, and unfortunately for Tracy, it took more than a harsh look to dissuade me from anything.

"Morning, Tracy," I said, leaning against the counter. "You and Lola must be really close."

"She's a dog. How could you not love her?" Tracy's face was deadpan. She had me there; I couldn't resist a dog, either.

"How long ago did Sylvia get her?" I asked, rubbing Lola's ears. There hadn't been a dog at the inn when I was a kid, and I wasn't even sure if Sylvia liked dogs.

"Three years," Tracy said, increasing the tapping on her keyboard. "What do you want?"

Okay, looks like we're done with that conversation. Clearly, her gentleness with Lola didn't extend to me. I leaned back from the front desk to give her a little space and thought about how to approach this conversation.

"It's crazy what happened yesterday, isn't it?" Not exactly a smooth segue.

"Yes, it's not often rich socialites end up dead at the inn," Tracy said, keeping her eyes on her computer. "I'm shocked you're still here, given everything that's happened."

"The police may still want to ask me some questions since I found her body and all. Besides, I still need to work with Ron to figure out what we're doing with the inn."

"I heard about Tony Vasco's offer. I always thought he was an idiot, but I didn't think he'd let a murder investigation get in the way of him claiming another property for his B&B empire."

What did Tracy think about Sylvia selling the inn to Vasco? She clearly didn't think highly of the man, but was she upset with Sylvia about it? Would Vasco replace all the staff here with his own employees?

I pushed the thought of Tony Vasco out of my head. The best thing I could do right now was figure out who killed Bethany.

"Did the police talk to you already?" I asked

"Yes," Tracy said with a small grimace. "Chief Tate has no idea what he's doing. They should bring in some actual detectives from Seattle."

My eyebrows lifted at her words. I'd thought Detective Patel had seemed competent, but maybe I was wrong. What did Tracy have against the chief of police?

"Gotta say, it's pretty unnerving to have a detective ask you if you have an alibi."

Tracy chuckled. "Seriously? They asked if you had an alibi? What, they thought you killed Bethany and pretended to find her body or something?"

"Right? Maybe they have to ask everyone. Did they ask you?"

"Yes. I was here late, finishing up some paperwork, then I went home. I live alone, but I'm sure one of my neighbors saw me return. This town is too nosy for its own good."

I chewed over what she said. Even though I didn't watch very many cop shows, I knew that being home by yourself wasn't a very good alibi. Was it possible the police suspected Tracy? She had gotten into an argument with Bethany the day before she died.

However, it would be pretty dumb of her to kill someone in her place of work. She'd be the number one suspect, after me, the person who found the body. Besides, being cranky didn't make you a murderer. What I needed was actual evidence.

"I'm sure the police will do whatever is best for the case,"

I said. Tracy grunted and kept her eyes on her computer. Maybe a different strategy made sense here.

"Did you know Bethany well?"

Tracy shrugged. "Not really. She was working on the charity auction, so we interacted while planning the event, but we weren't close friends. And as you saw, we didn't exactly get along."

"Yeah, from what I saw, she seemed like a real handful."

Tracy laughed, but there was no joy in it. "Tell me about it. A couple of weeks ago, she demanded that we keep all references to children out of the charity auction. Leaving out children from a charity event that benefits a children's organization, even pictures and advertisement? She said it would make the event seem juvenile. She didn't seem to understand the irony."

"What kind of person would do that? It's like she didn't want the kids getting in the way of her big event."

Tracy held her hands out, palms up, in a *who knows?* gesture. "That was Bethany for you."

"Speaking of the event, I'd love to help however I can. I haven't really planned charity auctions before, but with Sylvia gone, and now Bethany, I'm sure there's a lot of work to be done."

"I think I can handle it. If I need to make a cocktail, I'll be sure to give you a call."

Ouch. Did she think that was the only thing I was good for? Of course, I did make a good cocktail; Antonio and the other bartenders had taught me well, but still. I could do other things, too! Like find a killer.

"Do you know why Bethany was at the inn so late?" I asked, trying to think of a question that'd make her open up to me.

"No idea." Tracy flicked her eyes in my direction, then

back to her computer. "It doesn't really make any sense. If she'd been here for charity auction business, she would've told me she was coming by. But I don't know why else she would have been here, though I'm not surprised she got in. We don't keep things locked up as tightly as we should. We'll definitely start locking things up now."

She shivered a little, and I wondered if she was more uncomfortable with Bethany being in Sylvia's office than she was letting on.

"That's a good idea," I said with a nod. Something occurred to me. "I remember seeing you here that morning, before I found Bethany. You didn't go back to Sylvia's office?" When Ron had said she oversaw the day-to-day operations, I had figured that meant she'd use the office.

Tracy shook her head. "I do most of my paperwork up here. Checking orders and supplies, making sure the schedule is set up for the week. We can't have guests double-booking rooms, and we need to make sure there's enough staff working each day to manage everything. I don't really spend much time in Sylvia's office."

That made sense. She and Sylvia had been in charge of very different things, so it made sense that she wouldn't go back to her office. She also hadn't told me anything about Bethany I didn't already know, and she didn't seem likely to want to share much more. I had to figure out some way to breach her walls. Maybe honesty was the right move here.

"I totally understand what you're saying." I moved into her line of sight so she couldn't help but look up at me. "Honestly, I'm pretty freaked out by everything that's happened and trying to get answers. I want to find out what happened to Bethany, or at least try to help the police figure it out. When you inherit an inn, you start to feel responsible for the place."

Tracy put her hands on her hips. "You start to feel responsible for the place? Honey, you've been here less than two days. It takes more than that to know what this inn really needs. Do you even know the first thing about running an inn?"

She had me there. I was out of my depth with this place. Why did I think I could take over for Sylvia?

After a few moments of silence, Tracy spoke again. "If you're trying to figure out what happened to Bethany, you should talk to her husband." Her face was guarded, but there was something of a spark in her eyes. I'd almost forgotten she was still standing here.

"They weren't exactly happy," she continued, lowering her voice. "I probably shouldn't say any of this, but I know they'd been getting into big fights recently. I'm sure the police already have him on some list, but I bet that's where you'll get answers to your questions."

She sighed, looking pained for a moment. "Their house is on Clement Street, just past Roberts Avenue" she went on. "The big Victorian with the wraparound porch. Don't tell anyone I sent you." She sharpened her tone with that last sentence, and I knew I wouldn't tell a soul.

I turned away from the desk, my spirits lifted. I had my first clue!

12

The next morning, I rang the doorbell of the large Victorian and glanced over my shoulder. The rain had picked up, and I was grateful for the awning on the wraparound porch. I hadn't had a chance to buy a raincoat, and all I had to use was the dinky airport umbrella. I could feel the dampness at my ankles.

I'd considered telling Estelle and Miles about what I'd learned from Tracy and bringing them along today, but I had a feeling this man would be less willing to talk to the nosy senior citizens. I didn't want to spook him.

I turned back to the front door as it was opened by the man of the house. "Victor Stevens? My name is Simone Evans. I was hoping to speak with you about your wife. Could I have a few minutes of your time?"

Moments later, we were settled in his living room, and I studied the man across from me as he poured two cups of tea. I was surprised that he'd let me in so easily, but then I noticed the dark circles around his eyes. This man looked like he hadn't been sleeping and could be talked into anything.

Victor was tall and broad in the chest, with pale skin. His hair was cut short and, as he bent over the table to pour my tea, I noticed a bald patch at the back of his head. I put him in his fifties, at least, and I was certain Bethany wasn't a day over thirty-five. I took a sip of my tea as I processed that information.

"Thanks for coming by," he said, settling in across from me with his own teacup. "I hadn't realized that Sylvia had a niece. How long have you been in town?"

"Just a few days. I am sorry about what happened to your wife."

He dropped his eyes from mine and his face reddened. "Thank you. I still can't believe it. You think you have all the time in the world. You never imagine..." He broke off then, his voice catching in his throat, and I looked around the room to give him a moment to collect himself.

The space was well-decorated and looked expensive. Neutral tones, sleek lines, large paintings on every wall. It matched perfectly with the image of Bethany I'd built in my mind.

However, looks could be deceiving. What secrets might be hiding under the surface of this tidy home? Was Bethany truly happy with this man, twenty years her senior?

"Sorry about that." Victor had composed himself, and I gave him a tiny smile, taking another sip of my tea. Why, exactly, did I sign up for interrogating grieving widowers? Maybe I should've told Miles and Estelle and had them do this.

"You said you wanted to talk about Bethany?" Victor asked.

"Yes," I said, leaning forward. "I know my aunt would be grief stricken that this happened to Bethany, especially at the inn. I'd like to get to the bottom of this for Bethany's sake and to ensure the safety of our guests. What can you tell me about her?"

"She was a beautiful woman," he said, smiling and staring off at a spot over my shoulder. "We met about ten years ago. I'd moved to town to start the new manufacturing firm—we have offices all over the U.S., and globally, and Pine Brook was our next acquisition. Bethany was living with her mother at the time, caring for her while she battled cancer. She didn't make it. Instead, we fell in love."

"Sounds like you two were meant to be."

Tears hovered in his eyes. "I'll be honest with you, Ms. Evans. My wife and I had a good marriage for a long time, but it wasn't what I would call perfect. She'd been closed off recently. I couldn't tell why. It felt like she was pulling away. She'd gotten busy with her charity work, and I was opening another office for the firm in Vancouver, so I was gone a lot for work. I worried that we'd gotten used to each other. We didn't appreciate each other anymore. But I always thought we'd have time to get the spark back. I never expected..." He broke down then, burying his face in his hands and sobbing.

I patted his arm, watching this man grieve for his wife. Tears pooled in my eyes, watching this display of sadness and pain, and I took some deep breaths to steady myself.

Tracy had heard that Bethany and Victor were getting into big fights, but this man in front of me appeared genuinely heartbroken over what had happened to his wife. Maybe they were fighting, but he might've also truly loved her.

If Bethany was pulling away, did that give Victor a reason to want to kill her? I suppose it depended on why she was pulling away.

I looked around the room, giving him another moment

to collect himself. The living room was flawless; sleek lines, white furniture, gleaming surfaces. It was clear they didn't have children. My sister was the most glamorous person I knew, and the second she had her daughter, her house was never the same.

There were no photos on the walls. No clutter on the coffee table. Not even a TV propped up anywhere. Who designed this room? Did Victor and Bethany relax in here after a hard day at work? I couldn't picture it.

"Sorry about that." Victor dabbed his cheeks with a napkin.

"Don't apologize," I said quickly. "You're going through something challenging right now. I'm so sorry for bringing all of this up." I was getting more and more convinced that he had nothing to do with Bethany's death. His tears felt too real.

"I want to do whatever I can to find Bethany's killer," Victor said, waving away my apology. "Please, whatever you think might help."

I felt pain for this man, but I had to get through my questions if I had any hope of helping the police. "Have you spoken to the police?"

He nodded. "They came to me after you found her body. A woman detective came by, and I could tell that she thought I was involved." He smiled wryly. "It's practically a cliché, isn't it? Suspecting the victim's husband? Anyway, she had a lot of questions for me, wanting to know where I was when Bethany died and if we were having any problems." He shot me a resolute look. "I told her the same thing I told you, that I could tell Bethany had been pulling away. I didn't know why. I wish I did. I asked her, once, if everything was okay, but she just said that I was so busy with my work, it must seem like she was the one never around. She always knew how to turn things back around on me like that."

"It happens in all relationships at some point, doesn't it? We pull apart, then we find our way back."

"I suppose...but now we don't have time to find our way back."

"I'm sorry." I swallowed a lump. "May I ask what you told the police about where you were when she died?"

"The truth: I was at my office. I'd been working late the past few weeks, finishing up a big project that's due next week. I'm the lead on the project, so I've been staying late. I was probably the only person in the building besides my secretary. She likes to stay late when I do, though I always tell her she should feel free to go home. I'm sure the police are going to talk to her at some point."

I nodded, taking another sip. Did his working late the past few weeks have anything to do with Bethany pulling away? Or had she been pulling away before this big project started? She'd claimed that he was busy and she hadn't done anything wrong, according to Victor, but that wasn't necessarily the truth. He could be lying to me.

I didn't quite know how to ask that question without offending him, so I held onto it. I might figure it out without having to ask him.

"Any idea why she was at the inn so late?" I set my teacup down and crossed my legs.

"No idea," Victor said, after thinking for a moment. "I know she's been putting in a lot of work on the charity auction. Maybe she was meeting someone there to go over some details. Her co-chair might have more information for you, though."

Tracy had been certain that Bethany would've told her if she were coming by for charity auction business, but was it possible Bethany was meeting her co-chair there? I made a note to follow up with the co-chair. Maybe they would have more information.

"What else can you tell me about her? How were things going with the charity auction?" I asked.

Victor smiled, staring out into the distance. "My wife loved planning events. I think she would've been an event planner if we hadn't gotten married when we did. Joining the board of the Art Center was one of the best decisions of her life. Everyone on that committee loved working with her, and she loved them just as much."

My eyebrows raised a notch. That wasn't the impression I'd gotten from Tracy, that people loved working with Bethany. I made another note to check in with the co-chair and see what her take on Bethany was.

Maybe Victor was right in his assessment of how the other people on the committee felt about Bethany, and Tracy just didn't like her.

"Well, thank you for talking with me." I set my teacup on the table. "I don't want to take up any more of your time. I'm sure you have a lot to take care of right now."

"Not at all, I don't mind. I very much appreciate you trying to get to the bottom of what happened to Bethany. She deserves justice. But...please be careful."

"Be careful?"

Victor started worrying his hands. "I wouldn't want you to put yourself in any danger. This town has a lot of secrets, and someone might not appreciate a newcomer poking around."

~

VICTOR DIDN'T SAY MUCH MORE after that. He led me out of the house and waved while I climbed into my rental car. I sat in the car without turning on the engine, mulling over our chat.

Was he including himself in his assessment of how people in town would feel about me asking around? I still had so many questions.

And the biggest one of all: did he kill his wife? I'd seen genuine emotion in that living room, but could his sadness be from guilt? Was Victor now grappling with the knowledge that he'd taken his wife's life?

I turned the car on and pulled away from the curb. The police could probably verify his alibi. Victor would stay at the top of my suspect list until I decided otherwise, but I needed to question everyone if I was going to find Bethany's killer.

13

The rain had picked up as I drove away. My soggy umbrella now sat next to me on the passenger seat. This would not cut it. I headed into town, hoping I could find a clothing store selling raincoats.

The downtown area of Pine Brook was quiet as I turned onto the main boulevard. I found a parking spot on the street and looked up and down the road.

A small boutique was less than a block away, across the street. My hair would be an absolute mess once I got outside, but I made a mad dash for the store anyway.

It was quiet inside; clearly, few people were out during a rainstorm. I smiled at the shop owner as I walked in and began browsing the racks.

"Abby, please tell me you got in those new boots. I can't keep wearing last season's pair!" called another woman as she entered the store.

She obviously knew the shop owner well and barely glanced in my direction as they picked up a conversation about the new boots. I flipped through some coats and peered at my sneakers, wondering if I needed a new pair of boots, too.

I found a couple good options for coats and took my favorite to the front of the store, where the other customer was examining a flashy pair of boots. She was about my height, with sleek brown hair cut to her shoulders, expressive eyes, and a kind smile. She was wearing grey slacks, a red blouse, and a matching grey blazer.

"All set?" the shop owner asked, as I set my options down on the counter.

"I think so," I said with a smile.

"Great," she said, ringing up my items. "This coat is really nice," she added, holding up the grey one I'd chosen. "It'll be perfect once it gets chillier up here. I haven't seen you around before. Are you new in town?"

"I'm Simone Evans. My aunt was Sylvia, at the Hemlock Inn."

"Oh, Sylvia, of course! My name's Abby Glen. I heard Sylvia had left the inn to a family member. It's great to meet you." She folded the jacket into a bag, a lock of curly blonde hair falling from her bun. "Will you let Tracy know we just got those jeans in stock that she was looking for the last time she was here? I tried calling the inn but couldn't get through."

"Of course. I didn't realize you knew Tracy."

She shrugged. "Everyone in town pretty much knows everyone else. Must be scary, what happened with Bethany. Camille here was pretty close to her," she added, gesturing over to the other woman in the store, who had set the boots on the counter to check out.

"Camille Abrams," she said, holding out her hand. "I was co-chair with Bethany. You and I will probably work close together to get this event on track."

This was the woman Victor had thought I should talk to! What good luck was this. I shook her hand and thought of how best to approach things. Camille leaned in to pay for her boots, and I caught a whiff of her perfume. How lovely, it smelled like oranges.

I paid for my items, and Camille and I walked out of the store together. "I'm sure this is weird," I said slowly, figuring honesty was easiest. "But I was wondering if I could ask you some questions about Bethany?"

Camille blanched. "Me? I doubt I'd have any information that would help you find Bethany's killer."

Were people already figuring out that I was trying to find Bethany's killer? I didn't want this getting back to Detective Patel.

"I'm just trying to learn more about Bethany," I said hurriedly. "And, since you two worked together so closely, I thought you might be able to help. Her husband suggested I reach out to you, actually."

Camille paused at my words, lines creasing her forehead. "Really? Victor told you to talk to me?" She studied me for a moment, then nodded. "All right. Why don't we go to Cuppa Joe's?"

Fortunately, the coffee shop was around the corner, and the rain had slowed down. We grabbed some drinks and took a seat at the back of the shop. It was quiet in the afternoon, a few tables taken up by other patrons reading books or staring out at the rain. My tension eased just from sitting in the coffee shop.

"How is Victor?" Camille asked once we were situated at a table. "This must be so hard on him. I can't imagine losing a spouse so young."

"I think he's holding up as best he can. You said you worked with Bethany on the charity auction?" I hated to pry.

I didn't want to make anyone feel worse, but I wanted to do what I could to help solve this murder.

A chill went through me as I was reminded, again, that I'd found a dead body. Bethany's lifeless, milky eyes weren't going to get out of my head for a long time.

"Yes, we were co-chairs. I figured you'd want to talk about the event since we'll now be the ones planning it."

"I did want to talk to you about the event. I can't stop thinking about what happened to Bethany, though. It's so wild to imagine. Did she have a lot of enemies?"

"Ha. I'm not sure how to answer that." Camille sat back and crossed her hands over her lap. "It's not right to speak ill of the dead, I know that. I don't know if I'd say that Bethany had a lot of enemies, *per se*, but she could be difficult to work with. We'd been friends for years, all the way back to high school, and I've gotten used to navigating her overbearing personality."

She paused, taking a sip of her drink. "I know some other folks in town feel differently about her. She was so good at her job, though. She could put on any event you needed, with minimal prep and setup time, and everyone would consider it a success. Some of the other board members didn't enjoy having to work with her, but they couldn't deny her results."

Maybe Bethany had pissed someone off enough that they'd decided to kill her. "That's too bad. Did any of them complain about her to you?"

"Not directly. Bethany had an assistant who I'm sure hated her job. We could often hear Bethany yelling at the poor girl, saying she'd messed up some order or was incompetent at her job. I don't know why Angeline continued working for her, but she must've thought it looked good on her resume."

An overworked and under-appreciated assistant would probably have many reasons to want to kill her boss. I made a mental note to ask Estelle and Miles where I could find this Angeline.

"How long have you two worked together?" I asked.

Camille tilted her head, thinking. "Oh, at least five or six years at this point, planning different charitable events in the area. Like I said, we go way back. I knew Bethany in high school. We both went away to college but ended up back here. Everyone was pretty surprised when she ended up with Victor."

"How do you mean?"

"Well, I don't mean to gossip," she dropped her voice lower, "but it's practically town news at this point. Bethany was raised by her mom, who worked two jobs but never could make ends meet. She and I were friends because we liked all the same things, but we were from different social classes. Once she got together with Victor, it was like everything changed. She suddenly had the money to create the type of lifestyle she'd always wanted, and she did. Victor didn't seem to mind the way she tore through his credit cards, or at least he never complained to anyone. Who knows what happens behind closed doors? Maybe he was unhappy with her shopping addiction?"

I sat back, trying to reconcile this with the image of the man I'd met that morning, who'd seemed so in love with his wife. If you felt that strongly about a person, you probably wouldn't mind if they spent all your money.

"Do you think they were happy?" I asked Camille.

"From what I could tell, yes," she said with a nod. "But it's so hard to know. Bethany never said anything about it to me, but I know that her image was important. I'm not sure if there was anyone in her life she was honest with, you know?"

I nodded, filing all of this information away. Camille's perception of Bethany's marriage didn't quite match up with the image that Victor had painted for me that morning, but that didn't mean that either of them was lying. Sometimes relationships looked one way on the outside and another from the inside, but neither version was bad.

"Did she seem different at all in the weeks before her death? Worried about something, or unhappy?" Maybe the threat against her life had been building for a while, and the killer had finally struck.

Camille thought for a moment, tapping her pink fingernails against her bottom lip. "Now that you mention it, I do think she was upset last week. She wouldn't tell me what was wrong, but we had a meeting one day, and she showed up flustered and all out of sorts. I saw her again a couple days later, and she was totally fine again. She didn't even seem to remember how she'd been before."

This was interesting. Had something happened to her to cause her to get upset like that? Did she get into a fight with Victor, or maybe with someone else? I filed this information away for later, too.

"Do you have any idea why Bethany was at the inn so late that night? The police say she was killed between nine and eleven."

"No clue. Maybe she was meeting Tracy to go over plans for the auction?"

I shook my head. "Tracy says she doesn't know why Bethany was there, either. We were both in other parts of the inn, but didn't hear her back there. Victor actually wondered if she was meeting you there to go over plans for the event."

"No, Bethany didn't like late meetings. We tended to get everything done by five P.M."

If she wasn't meeting her co-chair, and she didn't have plans to meet with Tracy, then why was Bethany at the inn? Were either of these women lying to me?

"Do the police have any theories about what happened?" Camille asked, interrupting my thoughts. "I'm guessing they talked to you since you found her body, and it happened at your inn. They asked me to come in for an interview later this week, but the person I spoke with wouldn't give any details over the phone."

Did the police want to talk to Camille because they suspected her of having malicious feelings about her co-chair, or were they interviewing everyone in Bethany's life?

I shook my head and answered honestly. "No clue. They are being tight-lipped about the whole thing. Do you know much about the detective on the case, Patel?"

"Not much. I know she's new in town. A detective, yes, but also a rookie. I'm surprised she got this case. We don't get very many murders, as I'm sure you can imagine, and there are a couple more senior officers on the force who I would have assumed would get the case. Maybe they're retiring or something. She's probably going to have her work cut out for her."

More information to file away. Patel hadn't seemed like a rookie when she'd questioned me, but what did I know? I did feel better about snooping around; someone so inexperienced could probably use all the help they could get.

"Well, thanks for sharing all of this," I said. "I can't imagine how hard it must be to think about doing all this work without Bethany, but I appreciate you sharing what you know."

"Of course," Camille said. "I'm sorry I couldn't be of

more help. I didn't know too much about what was going on in Bethany's life. We were so busy planning the event, we didn't have much time to talk about other things. I hope they find her killer soon. Bethany didn't deserve to die. She was so young; we were the same age. Plus, it's scary to think about someone out there who could hurt us."

"Do you think more people might be in danger?"

"Who knows? Remember to lock your doors."

A chill went through me at her words. Were any of us safe here?

Camille glanced at the time on her phone. "I actually need to get going," she said, standing. "Good luck with everything. I'll be in touch about the charity auction." She waved goodbye and left me to my thoughts.

Had whatever Bethany had been upset about led to her death? I wasn't any closer to finding her killer, though I did have a nice raincoat now.

14

The lobby was quiet when I entered the inn, and I spotted a guest reading a book in front of the fireplace. I waved hello to Nadia at the front desk as she tapped away at the keyboard.

We'd been introduced the day before. She helped at the front desk and with the cleaning when the cleaners weren't around. We'd talked briefly about her time at the inn and her responsibilities here, but she'd been quiet and seemed more interested in emailing her boyfriend, who lived overseas.

I didn't feel like interrupting Nadia, so instead, I looked around the rest of the lobby, debating where to go next.

Lola came out from behind the desk and gave my hand a lick. I rubbed her ears and smiled down at the beagle. After seeing her interactions with Tracy, it felt good to know that Lola would be taken care of by Tracy once I sold the inn, even if Tracy didn't want to admit how close she was to the dog.

Estelle and Miles burst out from the bistro, their eyes gleaming as they hurried over. "We have some updates on the case," Estelle said, practically bouncing in place. Miles at least had the decency to look a little concerned that others might hear what we were saying.

"Let's go into the courtyard," I told them, guiding them away from prying ears. What had these two amateur sleuths found so quickly? Lola trotted out after us and settled on her dog bed in the courtyard.

"So what did you learn?" I asked once we were situated outside.

"Well, my hair stylist's mother works at the police station, and she hasn't stopped talking about the case," Estelle said. "Apparently, the letter opener that the killer used didn't have any prints on it, not even Sylvia's or Tracy's from before. So the killer must've wiped down the weapon after killing Bethany."

That was a smart move on the killer's part. Would most people be able to think that clearly after murdering someone?

"Now tell us what you found," Miles said, leaning forward in his seat. I told them about talking to Victor and Camille, but that I hadn't learned very much.

"It's hard to know if people are even telling me the truth," I said. "Some people have nice things to say about Bethany, and others seemed to hate her. What did you two think?"

Miles and Estelle exchanged a glance, and Estelle shrugged. "We didn't like her all that much either, but she was just one of those people you had to work with some-times. I wouldn't say I'm surprised that she was killed."

"Estelle! You shouldn't say such things about the dead." Miles scolded his wife.

"You know I'm right. She was an awful person."

"Did you know her well?" I asked.

"As well as we know anyone in town," Miles said. "Which is to say, not that much. It's a small town, but we're not privy to all the secrets this place has. But we all knew about her reputation. I don't know why Tracy still agreed to put on the event at the inn after Sylvia passed. They'd already gotten into so many arguments during the planning process; it seemed like it'd be easier for Tracy not to do it here."

"Oh, come on, Miles, you know how much Tracy loves the art center. She'd never do anything to hurt those kids," Estelle said.

"What did you think of Bethany?" I asked Estelle.

She waved her hand flippantly. "Similar to what Miles has said. I thought she was a difficult person to interact with. Once, we were decorating the town square for the Fourth of July celebration, and Bethany spent fifteen minutes screaming at a group of us because we'd used the wrong streamers. We'd put up the baby blue streamers we found in the box of supplies, when apparently she'd explicitly told us to use navy blue."

"No one told her to cut it out?" I couldn't imagine someone yelling at a group of adults and not being told to stop.

Estelle shrugged. "We were all so used to her, most of us just ignored her. She did put on a good event, and we all benefited from the interest she brought to town."

None of this was news, so I changed tactics. "What about Victor? What do you think of him?"

"I was never that impressed by him, though everyone in town loves him," Estelle said. "His firm has brought a lot of jobs into Pine Brook, but I always thought there was something fishy about that man."

"What do you mean?"

She shrugged. "I don't know. I've never liked him. He seems too put-together, you know? It all seems fake."

I didn't know exactly what she meant, but I added it to the list of things I was learning.

"Oh, Estelle, look what time it is," Miles said, holding out his wristwatch so his wife could see. "We need to get to dinner!" Miles turned to me. "Sorry for rushing off, but if we don't get in soon, we'll miss Pierre's freshest dishes."

I followed them back to the bistro, where Penny held open the swinging door.

"Hey Simone, coming in for dinner?" she asked, after Estelle and Miles had passed through.

I paused for a moment, thinking about all the info I'd been given and whether I wanted to sit around and eat. I wasn't ready yet. "Not right now. Just stretching my legs a bit. How are things in there?"

Penny shrugged with a laugh, tossing her long hair over her shoulder. "About what you'd expect right now. I'm sure Pierre will save something for you if you decide you want to eat later." She gave a tiny wave and stepped back into the dining room.

With no concrete plans, I headed back to Sylvia's office. The police had opened it back up for us, so I was hoping for some peace and quiet.

"Back so soon?" Tracy was in Aunt Sylvia's office, reviewing some documents. She sat on the lounger in the room, not behind the desk. I turned my back to where I'd found the body, a shudder tearing through me. Clearly we both weren't yet over what I had discovered at that desk the day before if we were avoiding it like this.

My gaze fell on another glass jar full of stones, this time on the windowsill. It hadn't been there when I'd been in here before. Had someone—maybe Tracy?—pulled it out of a drawer?

Tracy's tone was less argumentative than it had been previously, but I still wasn't interested in tiptoeing around her. Maybe she had more information she could share.

"What can you tell me about the Children's Art Studio?" I asked. "What did Bethany do for them?"

Tracy frowned. "She didn't *do* anything for them—she ran the whole thing. Why are you interested in that?"

"Just something her husband said. What can you tell me about it?"

"The Children's Art Studio has been around for a long time, in Holliston, the next town over. Bethany was on the Board of Directors, along with a few other organizations in the area. It seemed like her entire motivation in life was working with charities. Though, she wasn't the most charitable in her personal life. The charity auction brought in more visitors and the Holliston hotels always filled up, so that business usually spilled over to Pine Brook and helped us stay booked."

"What did my aunt think of the organization?"

"She felt similarly to me. It gave us more guests, but Bethany hasn't been a treat to work with this year. We loved the kids that it benefited. Art is important, and we were glad we could take part. I don't know what will happen with the event this year now that she's dead. Her assistant is coming by later this afternoon to discuss the next steps. It's a lot of work to plan, and I'm not sure how I'm going to do it all without Sylvia's help."

She dropped her head then and took some deep, calming breaths. What exactly was her relationship with my aunt? They worked together, of course, but was it more than that? It was sad to lose anyone, but was there more going on between them than I realized?

"I'd be happy to help—"

A thunderous sound erupted from the lobby, followed by a flurry of voices. Tracy leapt from the lounger and whizzed past, with me close on her heels.

The double doors in the entryway of the lobby flew open as men in overalls rolled in round tables. They rumbled over the wooden floors, coming to rest against the wall near the door, where six others were already stacked.

Nadia stood with her hands on her hips, a look of confusion on her round face. Lola briefly craned her neck around the side of the desk then settled back down in her bed.

"What's going on here?" Tracy's commanding voice caught the attention of everyone in the lobby.

One of the men in overalls held up a clipboard and flipped through the pages. He was tall and round, with a thick head of hair and a pink nose. "We've got a delivery for twenty tables for Bethany Stevens. Where would you like us to put them? This little one wasn't very helpful."

He gestured towards Nadia, who looked like she was regretting ever letting the tables into the building in the first place.

"We're not expecting an order of tables," Tracy said. "I think you have the wrong address."

"Nope, says right here, twenty tables to the Hemlock Inn, ordered by Bethany Stevens," the man said, pointing to his clipboard and holding it out to Tracy so she could read.

Tracy's eyes skimmed the clipboard and widened in surprise. "You're right. Bethany put in this order at the beginning of the year."

"You heard the lady," the man said, calling out to his

crew. "Bring in the rest." They jumped into action at his command.

"Wait, wait, you can't bring those in here," Tracy said, stepping in front of the man. "We don't have anywhere to put them right now."

"Not our problem." The man scribbled on his clipboard and tore out a sheet of paper. "Here's your receipt," he said, handing it to Tracy. "Nice doing business with you."

We watched him leave, helpless, as twenty tables were wheeled into the lobby of the inn. Tracy sighed and looked around. "I actually miss Bethany right now."

"I came as soon as I could!" An Asian woman came through the doors of the inn, dodging the tables being wheeled in. She was in her twenties, with a short pixie haircut and wearing a grey sweater dress.

"Angeline, thank goodness you're here," Tracy said. "Can you please take care of these tables?"

"I'm sorry," Angeline said, cringing. "There's nowhere else to put them. Bethany normally has them delivered to the location of the event the week before. I completely forgot about the shipment and tried to tell them she died so we didn't want them now, but they were already heading over here by the time I got on the phone. Isn't there anywhere we can put them here?"

"There's no space." Tracy held her arms out wide. "We haven't cleared out the dining room or anything yet for the event. It's not for days."

Angeline's eyes widened as she looked around, trying to find a solution. Something needed to be done about this, and quick.

"Can't you stick them in the corner?" I asked, piping up for the first time since we'd come out of the office. I cringed as soon as the words left my mouth. It was not a helpful suggestion.

Tracy's eyes flashed over to me, and Angeline noticed me for the first time. "Hello there," she said, holding out her hand. "I'm Angeline, Bethany's assistant—I mean, former assistant." Her shoulders hunched as she corrected herself, the reality of Bethany's death hanging over all of us.

"Simone," I said, shaking her hand and shooting her a tiny smile. I eyed her carefully. This must be the assistant Camille had mentioned. I hated to intrude on someone's grieving, but was there a chance I could speak to her alone?

I turned back to Tracy, wanting to be of help. "What about the courtyard? That's at least out of the way of the guests."

Tracy turned to me, no smile in sight. "I've got this under control. Why don't you run off and bother someone else?"

"I want to help," I insisted. "You've got a lot going on here. Why won't you let me help?"

"Because I don't want your help," Tracy said, her words clipped and her tone dangerous. "Just because Sylvia thought it would be a funny joke to leave this place to you, doesn't mean I have to work with you. I think it's best if you leave."

My mouth dropped open at her words. Who did she think she was?

"Whether you like it or not, we're going to have to work together." I gave her a firm look, then walked away, too aggravated to put up with her hostility anymore.

15

I got in line at Cuppa Joe's and put in my order. The coffee shop was busier in the evening, and I made sure to stick to herbal tea so I wouldn't be wired all night. Two visits to the same coffee shop in one day was excessive —even for me, lover of all things caffeinated—but I didn't know where else to go in town, and at least here I could sit down and think.

What was Tracy's deal? I sent a thought out into the universe. *Sorry, Aunt Sylvia, I know you hired this woman as your general manager, but I draw the line at verbal abuse!*

A couple people in the coffee shop recognized me, smiling when I made eye contact, and I returned their greeting. I was used to coffee shops in Los Angeles where no one went more than twice and everyone kept their eyes on their phones. This was a nice change of pace, as long as I could ignore Tracy's aggression.

At that moment, the door to the coffee shop burst open, letting in a rush of cold air as Angeline shuffled in. She looked as glamorous as she had at the inn. She and Tracy must've finished up whatever they were working on.

As Bethany's assistant, she could probably give some insight into the woman. Stumbling onto suspects like this was going to make this whole investigation thing go much easier.

I waited until she'd ordered her coffee, then sidled on over. "Angeline? Do you have a minute to chat?"

Her smile was warm, and I took that as a positive sign.

I walked her over to one of the tables. "It's so crazy, what happened," I said, once I'd given her a chance to take a sip of her drink. "I can't believe what happened to Bethany. Were you two close?"

Angeline slowly nodded. "I'd worked for her for five years, but I'm not sure if she was close to anyone. So you're taking over the inn?"

"I've just gotten to town, so I don't know exactly what I'm doing here. Finding a dead body wasn't part of the plan, that's for sure," I added jokingly. Angeline smiled but kept her gaze down. All right, noted—no more jokes about her dead boss.

"Losing her has got to be shocking for you. How was Bethany as a boss?" I asked, turning serious. "I met her briefly, the day before yesterday. She seemed...particular about what she wanted."

Angeline smiled. "That would be an understatement. But I loved working for her. I think she hired me mostly to make her lunch reservations, but she's so heavily involved in philanthropy, and it's been good exposure for me. She taught me so much. I wouldn't be where I am today if it weren't for her." Suddenly, her eyes filled with tears and she hunched over in her seat.

I patted Angeline's shoulder as she sniffled, ignoring the looks we were getting from the other tables. If Angeline was comfortable crying in front of everyone at the coffee shop, I wouldn't stop her.

Since Bethany was awful to work with, part of me questioned if Angeline was putting on a show for me. Why would she lie? People grieved in different ways, and it wasn't my place to tell her she shouldn't be crying about her boss. Still, I was dealing with a killer; I didn't know what I could trust.

"I'm sorry," she said, straightening. "It's still pretty fresh."

"No, that's okay." I passed her a napkin to dab her nose. "I had heard from some other people that Bethany was actually pretty hard to work with, but it sounds like you really enjoy working for her."

Angeline had the decency to blush and smile ruefully. "Well, I'm not sure if I'd go that far," she admitted. "She could be difficult sometimes. Once, we were planning an event in Seattle and I got food poisoning before we were supposed to leave for the event. Bethany decided I was faking it and forced me to get in the car with her. We were barely outside of Pine Brook when I threw up in her car and she made me take a cab back home."

"That's awful!"

"Yeah, I guess, but sometimes people have so much genius going on inside, it makes them more difficult to work with."

I doubted Bethany was truly a "genius" event planner, if that was even a thing. It sounded like she relished ordering other people around. But I kept my thoughts to myself.

"Do you know much about the event happening at the inn?" I asked. "It sounds like Tracy still wants to move forward with it, and I don't know much about it."

"It's a big deal. Normally Holliston puts it on, and Pine Brook gets some benefit from being close by. Since we're putting on the event this year, it's going to have a big impact on all the businesses in town. Though with Bethany gone, I don't know how things are going to go this year."

"Are you involved with the planning?"

"Yes, so I should probably have more confidence in the event's success this year," she said. "It's crazy to think about doing all of this without Bethany. She was such a big presence in this town; I don't know how we're going to fill that hole. I've got so much paperwork to get through in our office. I haven't really been able to spend much time there since Bethany died, but I know I'll need to go back, eventually."

I thought back to what Victor had told me about Bethany pulling away in recent months. Her assistant might've noticed something too.

"Had you noticed her seeming closed off, or like she was dealing with something at home?"

"Not really," she said. "Bethany didn't come to me with her problems or anything. I didn't notice any changes in her recently. Why are you so interested in all of this, anyway?" she asked, cocking her head to the side and narrowing her eyes, as if realizing that she was baring her soul to a stranger. Was she regretting being honest with me?

"I guess I'm still rattled about someone losing their life at the inn. I can't get the image out of my head, and I'm trying to wrap my head around who could've done this to her."

"I know, it's crazy to think about. I've been thinking about that too, you know? Wondering if it was someone from out of town, looking for someone to kill. Or if it could've been someone Bethany knew? They do say most killers know their victims."

I wondered where Angeline had gotten that little fact,

but didn't say anything. I guess I couldn't fault someone for their knowledge of true crime when my sister was an expert, too.

"Have the police talked to you yet?" I asked. "I imagine they'll want to talk to everyone in Bethany's life."

Angeline nodded. "This morning. They came by my place. It was so weird getting interviewed by the police. They kept asking me all these questions like they thought I had something to do with it."

My ears perked up then. "Really? Like what?"

"Just where I was when she was killed, the last time I'd seen her, stuff like that. But they really focused on where I was that night, like in a way that felt almost aggressive, you know?"

I paused, holding my breath, quickly thinking through the most casual way to ask my next question.

"What did you tell them? About where you were that night?"

"The truth, duh," Angeline said with a laugh. "I was staying with my parents. Sometimes my mom will cook dinner and I'd stay the night rather than going all the way home. They live in Holliston, and I don't like driving at night."

I took a sip of my tea to buy myself some time, thinking about what she had said. I could understand why the police were interested in her alibi. Parents would probably do anything to keep their child safe. Had Angeline snuck away and shoved a letter opener into her boss's chest?

She'd said that Bethany had helped her get where she was today, but did she secretly harbor ill-will towards the woman and had taken her vengeance that night? Had Angeline finally snapped? Had something driven her over the edge?

As much as I wanted to convince myself that Angeline had a clear motive, I had to admit that it was fuzzy, at best. If Angeline had snapped and finally stabbed her boss after years of mistreatment, wouldn't she have stabbed her more than once?

I wasn't a coroner or a doctor, but I didn't think I'd seen many stab wounds. Just the one, with the letter opener still sticking out of her chest. This murder also felt pre-planned; the murderer had lured Bethany to Sylvia's office at a time when few people were around. Was Angeline more conniving than I gave her credit for?

"That is crazy," I said, realizing I'd been silent for too long. "But it sounds like they left without arresting you, right? I mean, you wouldn't be here if they thought you were guilty."

"Yeah, I think that's true. They didn't have much else to say after my parents swore up and down that we'd been together that night. I mean, it's the truth, so I don't know why they kept focusing on it. Then they wanted to know more about the event happening at the inn and who was involved in planning it. I think they'll probably talk to those people next."

I'd follow up on Angeline's alibi with the police later. "Do you have any idea why Bethany was at the inn so late? I have to assume she was there because of the charity auction, but who would've met her there so late?"

Angeline shook her head. "No idea. I thought that was weird, too, when the police told me. Bethany did most of her work during the day. In fact, she hated having to go anywhere for work after five P.M. She must've had a good reason to be there so late." Angeline stared down into her mug, falling silent again.

Camille had said the same thing about Bethany not working in the evenings. So why was she at the inn?

"What about her husband? Were she and Victor happy?"

Angeline shrugged. "Like I said, Bethany never shared much with me. I got the impression that Victor liked having someone pretty to hang around him. Bethany never seemed to mind it, especially when she got a new purse out of it."

That wasn't exactly the impression I'd gotten from Victor, although their beautiful home did make me think he liked having nice things around him. What would he say if he heard this impression of his marriage?

Then I remembered what Camille had told me that morning. They both had the same opinion of Bethany and Victor's marriage: Bethany was just a trophy for Victor to parade around, but Bethany could buy whatever she wanted.

"Can you think of any reason someone would've wanted to kill her? I'm just trying to figure out how all this could've happened."

Angeline glanced around, as if checking to make sure that no one was eavesdropping, then leaned in close. I had a flashback to Camille doing the same thing in Cuppa Joe's this morning. People in this town sure did like their secrets.

"I probably shouldn't say this," she whispered, "but I think Bethany might've been blackmailing people."

I blinked at her words. "Blackmail? How do you know?"

Angeline looked around again, her eyes wide. "I overheard her on the phone once, threatening someone. I didn't hear who it was, but she told them she'd go straight to the local newspaper with what she knew if they didn't pay up. Maybe they killed her when they decided they didn't want to pay."

"Are you sure?" What kind of trouble had Bethany gotten herself into?

Angeline leaned back in her seat, as if regretting letting this slip. "I shouldn't say much else. I already told the police about it earlier. I thought you might want to know since it sounds like you're trying to figure out what happened to her."

"Oh, no," I said hurriedly. "I'm not trying to find her killer or anything." I couldn't let this rumor start going around town. The police wouldn't be happy with me, and the killer might decide to put a stop to me themselves. "I'm trying to make sense of what's going on. Do you know who Bethany might've been blackmailing?"

"I don't really know." Angeline shifted in her seat. Suddenly, she stood and backed away from the table. "The police told me to keep quiet about this, so I should probably go. Good luck finding the killer." She left Cuppa Joe's, pushing her way through the small crowd in the shop.

What had spooked her? Was she worried the police would learn she was telling people that Bethany was a blackmailer? Or was she worried about the killer overhearing her spilling their secret?

I SAT BACK against the chair after Angeline was gone, my thoughts whirling. While Bethany had seemed rude and hard to work for, could I really see her blackmailing someone? What kind of person would blackmail another person?

What could I do with this information? I could try to locate the person Bethany was blackmailing, but where would I even start? I couldn't just go around asking people if Bethany was blackmailing them.

Angeline claimed she'd already told the police about this, so I wouldn't be bringing them any new information. That assumed she hadn't been lying to me about telling them what she knew, which was always a possibility.

Angeline had mentioned she and Bethany had offices downtown; was there some way I could get into those and look for evidence of blackmailing? Angeline had seemed pretty freaked out when she left and I didn't think she was likely to let me in. I wasn't interested in trying to break into their office.

My best bet was to go back to the inn and see if I could figure out who Bethany was blackmailing.

16

The next morning, I came downstairs after another run in the area and spotted Nadia checking out a few guests. She'd mentioned before I left for the run that we weren't expecting anyone else to check in today, so things were quiet. I went back into the bistro to see if I could help there.

"You're a lifesaver," Penny said, passing me a rag when I asked if I could help. "Eddy's on break." She pointed me to a table that needed clearing and I got to work.

As I wiped up the table and stacked some dishes to bring into the kitchen, I thought about what I'd learned so far. Angeline's tip about Bethany blackmailing had been unsettling. I didn't think people actually blackmailed each other, but Angeline had been convinced.

The evening before, I'd stopped off at the police station after Patel had left me a message about taking my fingerprints. She hadn't told me anything useful about the investigation.

"Well, I think I'm going to stick around for a few days," I had told her, trying to seem nonchalant while she pressed my fingertips onto black ink. She didn't need to know I was doing any snooping.

"Be careful," she said, pressing my fingers to a pad to get the print. "There's a killer out there."

Back at the inn, lifting the stack of plates and glasses I'd made, I began weaving through the tables to the kitchen door. It annoyed me that I still hadn't figured out who or what had upset Bethany so much before her death, which Camille had told me about.

Whoever or whatever it was, it must hold the key to finding her killer. You don't get into arguments one day, get killed that same week, and not have it be related! But I didn't know how to figure out the truth.

Suddenly, my foot slipped out from under me as I slid through a puddle of water on the ground and the plates and glasses came crashing down around me. I blinked up from the floor, as the dining room quieted and everyone stared at me. I wished the floor would suck me right up, so I wouldn't have to face anyone after that fall.

Tracy groaned as she entered the dining room. "Here," she said, grabbing a broom from the closet and passing it to me. "Clean it up before someone slips."

She helped me up from the ground, then sighed and went into the kitchen. I reddened and followed her orders, ignoring the looks from the tables nearby.

"Simone! Are you all right?" I looked up from my sweeping to find Estelle in front of me, concern written across her face.

"I'm okay," I said, my voice still a little shaky. "Just a little slip."

"Here, let me help." Estelle grabbed the dustpan and expertly swept up the glass. I watched in amazement as she made quick work of the mess, carting everything off to the kitchen when she was done.

"Wow, thank you," I said, once she returned, surprised about how swiftly she'd moved.

"Don't worry about it," she said with a smile and a wave of her hand. "I spent my college years working as a server, and those skills don't go away." She studied me for a moment, going quiet. "You look like you could use a friendly ear. Miles is running an errand. Would you like to join me?" she asked, gesturing to her table, where she'd been reading a book before my fall.

I hesitated, still embarrassed by my trip.

"I ordered too many croissants. I need help getting through them." Estelle steered me over to her table and plopped me down in a chair. She pushed the warm pastry across the table to me, and I practically inhaled the croissant.

"Sylvia always loved sweeping the floors," Estelle said, ignoring my horrible table manners. "She said it reminded her of when she was a little girl and her mother let her sweep the floor with a broom twice her size. Technically, Penny and Eddy are in charge of keeping this place swept, but you could always find Sylvia in here, taking care of things herself."

I smiled, thinking about child-age Sylvia with a giant broom. My mom hated sweeping, so they must've been a good match when they were younger.

A woman with gray hair pulled back into a low bun walked up to our table. "Estelle, dear, how are you?" she asked, her blue eyes sparkling.

"Oh, Kathleen! Please sit with us. This is Simone, Sylvia's niece."

Kathleen turned her gaze on me. She was wearing a

sweater, slacks, and pearls. She was about eighty years old but looked like she could trick a kid into giving up his candy.

"How dreadful about your aunt, but I'm so happy to meet you," she said.

"I'm happy to be here," I said with a smile.

"A lot of drama happening here recently," Kathleen went on, looking back at Estelle. "A murder victim at the Hemlock Inn! What could happen next?"

"We've been talking about that," Estelle said in nearly a whisper. "Simone and I are looking for the killer."

"Estelle!" I hissed, annoyed that she was going around telling people about this, but Kathleen only laughed.

"Oh, Estelle, don't tell me you're getting involved in something else you shouldn't be involved in," she said. She turned to me. "This woman thinks everyone else's business is her business, and don't even try to tell her she's wrong. You should leave this to the police."

"That's what I tried to tell her, but she's very persistent."

Estelle stuck her tongue out at me at my words.

"I can't say I'm surprised it was Bethany," Kathleen went on. "She always had a habit of making people angry. Did I tell you about the screaming match last week?" she asked Estelle.

My ears perked up. "Screaming match? What do you mean?"

Kathleen put her palm over her heart and let out a little gasp. "Oh, I thought it was all over town. Estelle was visiting her sister in Seattle, so she didn't see it, but there were a few of us there, in the town square."

"What happened exactly?" I asked, leaning forward in my seat. Was this the thing that had upset Bethany that Camille had referred to?

"Some of us saw Bethany arguing with someone," Kathleen explained. "No one was close enough to hear what exactly they were arguing about, but it became very heated. Bethany was yelling in this man's face. I was worried someone was going to have to go in and break it up, but then he left pretty quickly."

"Do you know who she was arguing with?" I asked.

"He's new in town, just moved into those apartments by the water. Looks like trouble to me," Kathleen added, pursing her lips. She seemed more likely to cause trouble than this random visitor, but I didn't say anything.

"He doesn't seem to have a job, and no one knows why he's here," Kathleen went on. "I'd say he's a vagrant, unemployed and drifting around town, but he has a home, so I don't know what you'd call that."

What had they been fighting about? Had it been such a nasty fight that this mystery man had sought Bethany out after the fact and stabbed her in the chest? It must've been a loud fight to attract the attention of other people in the town square.

"What's his name? Has anyone asked him about the fight since Bethany's death?" The police had probably already talked to him, but could I figure out what they had learned?

To my surprise, Kathleen shook her head. "His name is Damian, but no one's seen him since their argument. I know, I've been asking around for him. I lead the town watch, and I wanted to make sure he hadn't gotten himself into any kind of trouble, but no one's heard from him in days."

This man may be the key to solving Bethany's murder. Why would he leave town after getting into a fight with her if he didn't have anything to do with her death?

I knew I was supposed to help at the inn, but I had a

feeling I was on the right path with this new person. I needed to figure out where he'd gone and try to get some evidence that he'd murdered Bethany and bring it to the police.

"Kathleen, do you know where this man lives?" I asked.

She nodded and wrote down his address. "These apartments are on the far side of town. I know his landlord. I'm not sure which unit he lives in."

I thanked her and stood, hurrying out of the bistro. I hoped Tracy and Nadia could handle things at the inn while I looked into this clue.

17

"**D**o you think anyone will be home?" Estelle asked.

She sat in the passenger seat, clasping her hands in her lap and buzzing with excitement. After I'd decided to go to Damian's apartment, Estelle had assumed she was along for the ride. I'd tried to convince her to stay at the inn, but she wouldn't listen.

"Haven't you seen any horror movies?" she had asked me. "You never go to the suspected killer's house alone. Especially not during a rainstorm!" She pointed out the window of the inn, and I had to agree that she was right.

It was the perfect weather for snooping around, though. Everyone would be bundled up inside, and no one around to see us tracking a killer.

Damian's apartment was in a part of town I hadn't been to yet. The building was three stories tall and looked to have six apartments on each floor. Kathleen hadn't known which apartment unit Damian had lived in, but I hoped they labeled the mailboxes with names.

Estelle hurried out of the car as soon as I came to a stop in front of his apartment. I sighed and spent a moment in the car, staring out the windshield. Were we really about to do this?

The rain was coming down even harder than it had been when we left, and I wrapped my raincoat tighter around my body. If I waited too long, Estelle would try to break into his apartment on her own. It was now or never.

I dashed out of the car and into the rain, making a beeline straight for the lobby. Estelle was inside, dripping all over the shag carpeting. The lobby was quiet and smelled of cigarette smoke. The carpet was threadbare and the walls could've used another layer of paint.

A light fixture flickered on the ceiling, battling with the gloom coming from outside to keep the lobby lit, and a sad fern sat in the corner.

Mailboxes lined the far wall, and we hurried over to them. They appeared to be in alphabetical order and all were labeled. I found Damian Miller's easily enough: 3B. I didn't see an elevator, so we trudged up the stairs.

We paused at the top of the stairs. The third floor was quiet, though I could hear a muffled TV coming through the door of one unit. How many people were home right now? Was Damian home?

What exactly was I looking for here? I wanted to talk to this man, to see if he knew anything about Bethany's death. Was it possible he killed her? I had to figure out what he was doing in town.

Estelle and I counted down until we got to 3B and I knocked. No answer. I knocked again. Still nothing. Estelle looked ready to kick the door in, but I motioned for her to stop.

I took a step back and thought about what we were doing. Was I really knocking on the door of a man I suspected to be a killer? I wasn't a cop or even an amateur detective, and this could easily lead to us getting killed.

I spun around, ready to hightail it back to the inn with my tail between my legs, and slammed into a wall of a man.

"Can I help you?"

I looked up at the giant I'd walked into. He was at least a foot taller than me, wearing a wife-beater with food stains down the front. His brown hair was long and scraggly, and cigarette smoke radiated off of him.

Of course Damian would be a walking nightmare. I gulped. Estelle gave a tiny squeak behind me and then she was hightailing it down the side stairs. I sighed as she abandoned me. So much for partners in crime.

"I said, can I help you?" the man repeated. He looked past me to the door behind and read the number on the door. "Are you looking for Damian?"

I let out the breath I hadn't realized I was holding. This wasn't Damian, which meant I wouldn't get killed. Probably. I eyed the man's muscles and wife-beater, and figured he'd seen his fair share of fights.

"I am," I said, taking a step away from him to put some space between us. Just because he wasn't a killer, didn't mean I wanted to stand so close to him. "I knocked, but he didn't answer. Have you seen him around?"

The man shook his head. "Not for a few days. I'm Martin, the landlord. I was doing my check of the halls. We get some nasty characters through these halls, so I like to keep an eye on things."

He eyed me in a way that made me wonder if he thought I was a nasty character, and I smiled, hoping to keep him from calling the police.

"Any idea where he might've gone?" I asked.

He shook his head. "He didn't say. I saw him packing up a bag and taking off in his car."

"When was this?"

"Oh, about three days ago. I didn't think to ask him where he was going. This isn't that kind of place. Why are you looking for him? Does he owe you money?"

I shook my head, processing what Martin had said. Three days was right after Bethany was murdered! Had Damian killed her and then fled town? Is that why no one could find him now?

"I'm Simone. I'm the owner at the Hemlock Inn. I understand Damian got into a fight with Bethany Stevens before she died. Do you know anything about that?"

"She came by here, looking for Damian. Before she died, I mean."

"Really?" I asked, my eyebrows shooting up my forehead. "When was this?"

Martin thought. "Oh, this past weekend, I think. I was fixing the pipe down the hall, and I saw her storm up the stairs and bang on his door. Just like you did. Except Damian was home that day, and he answered. Bethany started laying into him as soon as he opened the door, blabbing about him needing to stay away and leave her alone. Damian must've seen me standing in the hall, because he hurried her into his apartment real quick. From the way she was going on about him needing to stay away, I was surprised she went inside, but it's not any of my business."

"Did you tell the police this?" I asked, shocked at all he had shared.

"Why would I?" Martin said. "No one's come around asking questions. Except for you. Listen, if we're done here, I need to get back to the rest of the floors."

He left then, climbing back down the stairs and leaving me at Damian's door.

This changed things for sure. Not only had some towns-people seen Bethany arguing with a man a few days before her death, but Martin had seen her enter his apartment a few days before the murder.

While Martin didn't think Damian had forced her into the apartment, the way he described her temperament and what they were yelling about made me think Bethany may not have gone inside willingly. If Damian was already yelling at her before her death, it wasn't such a stretch that he might kill her a few days later.

I thought about Patel. She'd asked me to tell her if I had any new information, and this seemed pretty important.

At the very least, someone needed to talk to Martin about what he had seen with Bethany and Damian. The police were better equipped at figuring all of this out than I was.

The police station was across town, so I left Damian's apartment building and got into my car. Estelle was long gone, but I didn't care. I finally had a clue, and hopefully, this would get the police one step closer to solving Bethany's murder, so Tony Vasco would buy the inn.

18

The police department was in a large, redbrick building on the edge of town. Two stories tall, it was both squat and imposing. I sat in my car across the street, debating the merits of what I was about to do.

I'd wanted to call Detective Patel directly, but I'd left her card at the inn and didn't want to go all the way back to get it. Might as well get this over with.

The station's entrance opened onto a front desk with a glass window running its length, presumably to protect the person on the other side. Benches sat on either side of the front door, and I tried to ignore the handcuffs hanging from the ends of the benches, where a man currently slouched. His afternoon scotch radiated off him, and I held my breath as I walked past.

A man sat behind the glass window, looking like he'd jumped straight out of high school and right into law enforcement. He was pale, with dark brown hair cut close to his scalp, and he stared at his computer monitor, fingers moving lazily across the keys. He had a tiny red dot where he'd nicked himself shaving. A name badge identified him as Officer Collins.

I smiled as I approached the front desk, wondering how best to play this. I remembered Detective Patel then—maybe I should ask for her directly?

"Bail bondsman is located around the corner, next building over," he said before I could open my mouth. I frowned, wondering what about me made him think I was looking for a bondsman, but moved past it.

"I have some information about the Bethany Stevens case," I said, using my most commanding voice. "I was hoping to speak with Detective Patel about it."

"Detective Patel is out on assignment," he said. "You can leave a message and she'll get back to you once she has time."

I knew a brushoff when I saw one. I wasn't interested in waiting around for this twerp to give Patel my message if he ever did.

"Maybe you could give me her number," I said instead. "That way, you don't have to write anything down."

"Collins!" someone yelled. A loud bang sounded as a side door swung open, smacking against the wall. I jumped, and so did Officer Collins. Guess we were all a little jumpy today. Collins hopped out of his seat, coming to attention.

A man walked through the open door, his eyes roaming the front sitting area. He sneered as his eyes landed on the drunk in the corner, and the sneer deepened when he saw me standing at the front desk. I got the briefest of looks before he turned his attention to Officer Collins.

He was wearing a full uniform, with blonde hair beginning to thin and a gut that extended out past his toes. His name tag identified him as Chief Tate.

"Where are those notes on the Harrison burglary?" he asked Collins.

I took a step back, not wanting to give him any reason to turn his gaze on me. Clearly he was in some kind of mood, and I thought it best to stay out of his way. Maybe I should've waited around for Patel, or come back when I thought she'd be around.

"This lady has some information about the Stevens murder," Collins said.

I looked up, my eyes wide. Drat. I guess I wasn't going to get out of this one. Tate turned his critical gaze to me.

"Is that so?" he said, taking a step closer to me. "Well, out with it."

I ran through what I had to say, stumbling over my words under the imposing presence of this man. I told him about Damian and my suspicion that he'd killed Bethany. I could tell I was losing his attention and finished up.

"You're the one who found her body, aren't you?" Tate asked after a long pause. I nodded, unable to form any words under his harsh gaze.

"Why don't we step outside for a moment?" he said, his voice softer. Then he nodded his head toward the drunk. "Collins, keep an eye on this one, why don't you?"

He guided me outside of the police department, where the wind had picked up since I'd entered the building. I wrapped my jacket tighter around myself and turned to Tate, interested to see what he had to say.

"Now, you listen here," he said, leaning towards me and practically wagging his finger in my face. "This murder has nothing to do with you, and I won't have you running around, shooting your mouth on things you know nothing about. You're not a police officer, and we don't need your help. You stay out of our business now, you hear? Or I might have to bring you in on obstruction of justice. Tampering with witnesses is a crime. Understood?"

I nodded, too surprised by his outburst to say anything else. He narrowed his eyes at me once more, then stalked back into the building.

I stood staring at the road, shocked at his words. I hadn't expected that level of anger directed towards me. I wasn't sure what I had done to warrant it. All I was trying to do was help find a killer.

Tate wasn't the most welcoming person I'd met so far in Pine Brook, and, in fact, he might even be worse than Tracy. How did I find the crabbiest people in town?

"Simone? What are you doing here?"

Bracing myself for another barrage, I looked up at my name. Detective Patel was walking towards me, a hard look in her eyes. I didn't think she'd yell at me, but I wasn't sure if she'd be happy to see me.

I hesitated, then explained that I'd talked to Tate to share some news about the case. I skirted around his aggressiveness, as I didn't want it getting back to him that I'd been bad-mouthing him around town, but I could tell Patel didn't quite believe me.

"I haven't been working with Tate for long, but I'm sure it was worse than that," Patel said, a grimace on her face. "He's not a fan of civilians butting their heads into investigations. I can't say I am, either," she added, her tone stern, her hands on her hips. "We've finished our questions with you; I'm surprised you're still here."

My insides curdled, but I took a couple deep breaths. "I know, and I'm sorry. I'm not meaning to get in the way. I just... People keep telling me things, and I want to help find Bethany's killer." I wisely decided not to mention that I was asking those people questions in the first place.

Patel studied me for a moment, her eyes hard to read. She seemed to come to some decision. "Let's go inside. And you can tell me about these things people keep telling you."

She led me into the building through a side door, skirting around the chief and other officers. She brought me into a back room and we sat at a table while she took notes.

I explained what I'd learned, including the different alibis and ways I thought people might be lying, plus the information I'd picked up about Damian.

"I honestly thought Victor was telling the truth. He's an excellent liar if he wasn't. And if he was, then why did Angeline say what she did? Could she be hiding something? Plus, you need to look into Damian. He hasn't been seen since their argument, and his landlord, Martin, says no one has been around to question him."

I sat back, spent from all the information I'd shared, and waited for Patel to tell me how brilliant I was.

Patel studied her notes, her brow furrowed. "Tate is right. You're not a police officer and you're getting involved in something dangerous that doesn't concern you. I can't have you going around talking to suspects. You need to stay out of this. You could cause someone to get scared and leave town, or you might keep them from coming to the police with what they know. I don't want to arrest you for obstructing justice, but I will if you keep inserting yourself into an official police investigation. We'll send someone to talk to Martin about this Damian person, but that's all I'll say on the matter."

My heart sank at her words. I was so certain I was bringing her something important, but this entire trip had been a waste of time. Instead, I'd pissed off a detective and the chief of police. Go, me.

I promised to stay out of her way, though I didn't quite

believe that promise. Patel led me out of the station and watched as I got in my car and drove away.

Tapping my fingers against the wheel to the song on the radio, I thought about what she'd said. True, I wasn't a cop, and true, I didn't know what I was doing. But I'd gotten some good info out of some people. Plus, I'd found someone who might point directly to Bethany's killer, and the police hadn't even known about Damian in the first place.

Was I going to give up on my search for Bethany's killer? I needed to save the inn; I couldn't stop now. I just had to stay out of Tate's way and keep quiet about what I was doing.

Now, if only I could figure out how to keep something quiet in this town.

19

The next morning, I woke to rain pouring down from the sky in sheets. Lola and I went out on her morning walk like we had every morning since I'd arrived in town, but my raincoat and umbrella couldn't protect us from the showers.

After the walk, my jeans were soaked and unlikely to dry anytime soon. Lola shook herself when we got back to the inn, and most of the rainwater wicked off of her. Lucky dog.

The night before, I'd done a search online for Damian Miller. If the police wouldn't talk to me about him, then I had to find the answers myself.

I hadn't found much. It was a common name, so about fifteen different Facebook profiles popped up. I hadn't seen what he'd looked like, so I didn't know which was his. Hopefully the police were having better luck hunting him down.

After settling Lola onto her bed behind the front desk with a chew stick, I went to the bistro to check on things. The bistro was quiet, and everyone seemed to be settled in well. I spotted Nick chatting with Eddy and went over to say hello.

"Another delivery already?" I asked Nick.

He grinned. "Pierre loves his fresh produce. I usually come by a couple times a week."

Eddy turned to me, clapping Nick on the back. "Nick here is too modest. His produce is the best in a fifty-mile radius, and Pierre knows our guests would leave if we gave them anything else. He asks Nick to come so often to make sure we get the best of the best."

Nick laughed and rubbed the back of his neck, glancing down at the floor. "I don't know about that. I just know people seem to like what I grow."

"How long have you been supplying the bistro?" I asked him. Nick looked young, but I knew the bistro had been around for at least a decade. Was he older than I realized?

"The past four years, but before that, my dad brought in the produce."

"Oh...so it's a family business?"

"Yup. We've owned our farm for the past three genera-tions. My grandpa emigrated from Japan in the 1940s and picked up a plot of land not far from here. He expanded it to nearly twenty acres when he was alive, and my dad took over when he passed. My dad's been sick recently, so I've been taking over more and more of the work. One day, the entire farm will be mine to manage alone."

I smiled as he spoke. Who knew Nick could be so chatty?

"I'm sorry to hear about your dad," I said. I couldn't imagine managing an entire farm and caring for a sick parent. I could barely keep one job!

"Thanks. It's been tough, but we're managing." He glanced at the time on his phone. "I need to get going and drop off another shipment. Eddy, think about what I said about the team. I think it could be really good." Nick said goodbye and left us in the bistro.

"What team?" I asked, turning to Eddy, who'd gone back to counting up receipts.

"Oh, fantasy football," Eddy said, flapping his hand in Nick's direction. "He's always trying to get a team together this time of year, but I don't know why he keeps asking the gay guy to join. I mean, do I look like I care about football?"

I took in his spiked hair, that was now green today, his chunky black sweater, and his hands with about ten rings sprinkled throughout his fingers, and shrugged. "Maybe he thinks you'll like it."

Eddy rolled his eyes. "The only football I'm interested in is when a Swedish masseuse rubs the balls of my feet. I don't know how to make that any clearer to Nick."

I laughed. If Nick couldn't tell by now that Eddy was the last person to be interested in fantasy football, he was probably never going to figure it out.

"Have you heard anything else about the police's investigation into Bethany's murder?" Eddy glanced up from the receipts.

I shook my head, my ears still ringing from Tate's outburst. "Nothing they're telling me, at least."

"It's pretty scary to think about. I hope they figure it out soon. Who knows if the inn can handle something like this."

"What do you mean?"

"Well, I heard Nadia say we've already had some cancellations, and things have been quieter in the bistro. Aren't you worried people might not want to come here anymore?"

He was right; I'd had that same thought, but I hadn't wanted to admit it. Could the Hemlock make it through this murder investigation unscathed, or would everyone soon be out of jobs? I needed to find the killer to keep Tony Vasco's offer and save everyone's jobs.

Eddy was called over by a guest, so I walked out into the lobby and spotted Tracy at the front desk.

"Oh, there you are," she said as I approached. "Can you stay here and watch the front desk? I'm meeting Angeline at Bethany's office to pick up a list of VIPs for the auction. I'd prefer to stay here and out of the rain, but Camille and I need the names to finalize the guest list. Nadia is around if anything comes up," she added, grabbing her purse from behind the desk.

She was going to Bethany's office? I'd been hoping to see where Bethany worked and see if there was anything there that might lead to her killer. But could I convince Tracy to let me go instead?

"You're right; it is raining pretty bad out there." I moved so that I was blocking her way out from behind the desk. "Why don't you let me get it? I'm already pretty soaked," I added, gesturing to my jeans. True, they had dried some after my walk with Lola, but you could still see patches of damp on them.

Tracy narrowed her eyes. "You want to go instead? Why? It's boring charity auction work."

"I'd like to help with the charity auction. I know it's been a lot of work already, and it's probably hard to manage everything with both Sylvia and Bethany gone. Besides, how hard is it to pick up a list of names?"

Tracy didn't say anything for a moment, as if thinking it might be pretty hard for me to do something as easy as find a list of names, but then she shrugged and stepped back behind the desk.

"All right, fine, I won't stop you from getting soaked again." She grabbed a slip of paper and scribbled something on it, then passed it to me. "That's the address. Angeline will meet you downtown."

I snatched the paper away and hurried back outside before Tracy changed her mind. I had a feeling Bethany's office might hold some clue as to who had killed her, and I didn't want to miss out on this perfect opportunity to snoop. Hopefully, I could get Angeline to leave me alone for a few minutes while I looked around.

I met Angeline at a building downtown close to Ron's office. She explained that she and Bethany had been renting two offices in this building, as Bethany had felt that she needed the space to do her work.

"I wouldn't exactly call it work when all she was doing was chatting with her friends and planning the next big party," Angeline said, unlocking the front door and leading me back to Bethany's office. "But I appreciated the desk space. I'm not sure if you'll find what you need here. The police came through and took some things already." Her phone rang then, and she stepped outside to take the call, giving me some time alone.

Surprisingly, Bethany's office was a very cozy space. Much more welcoming than her home had been. Photos all around, with a wool blanket on the lounger in the corner. Did this cozy space mean Victor had designed their home?

I knew Tracy would expect me to come back with the list of VIPs for the party, so I looked around for that first. Nothing jumped out immediately. I didn't know how long Angeline was going to be gone for, but I didn't want her catching me snooping around her boss' office, so I locked the door and got to work.

There was an empty spot on Bethany's desk. I assumed the police had taken her computer, which meant I wouldn't be able to search it. Probably for the best. She more than likely used a password, and I wouldn't be able to break that on my own.

I began looking around the office, pulling open drawers and cabinets, looking for clues, all the while keeping my ears tuned to the office door in case anyone approached from the other side.

I couldn't find a single thing to shed light on who had killed Bethany, though I did find the list of VIPs in a drawer and stuck it in my pocket. Bethany kept the office clean, with few papers strewn about.

I figured she was probably the kind of person to do all of her work on her computer, which meant I wasn't going to find much in the office.

Discouraged and feeling like this was a waste of time, I flopped down in Bethany's office chair, trying to figure out what to do with the little time I had left. I leaned back and rested my head against the headrest, racking my brain to come up with a plan.

I let out a breath and rolled my eyes, glimpsing something odd about the paneling on the ceiling. It looked like something was poking out.

After listening for Angeline at the door, I climbed onto Bethany's chair and finally her desk to get me closer to the ceiling. I pressed against the ceiling tile and gasped as it opened, sliding to the side. I reached inside and pulled out a flat leather book.

With still no noise in the hall, I climbed down from the chair and set the book on the desk. Inside was a list of names in a spreadsheet. My eyes ran over the page as I tried to decipher the words.

I pulled out a used notepad from the drawer and compared the handwritten words on both documents. The handwriting looked the same. Why was Bethany keeping some kind of log in her ceiling?

Scanning down the page, I tried to understand what I was seeing. Each name had a number written in the next column, followed by a short description: "Paid in full," "Due next week," "Overdue," or some other notation. It looked like an accounting log. But why would it be in the ceiling?

I flipped to the next page in the book. On the second page, the names were repeated down the side, but the information in the next column was unexpected.

Cheating on his wife.

Photos of her stealing from her son.

Did that weird thing with the duck.

Each name had some action written down next to it. Why was Bethany logging these things?

The book slipped from my hands as a chill went through me. I knew what these notes meant. Hadn't Angeline told me that she thought Bethany was blackmailing people?

I hadn't totally believed her at the time, but now, with these dollar amounts written down and these descriptions that people would probably pay to keep secret—it was beginning to sound more reasonable.

At that moment, Angeline tried to open the office door, and I jumped, knocking the book off the table. I picked it up and shoved it into the back of my pants, pulling my jacket over the bulge. I wasn't going to leave this behind. I hurried to the door and unlocked it.

"Sorry about that!" I said, stepping out into the hallway and partially closing the door. "Lock must've slipped when I shut it."

Angeline was standing on the other side of the door, holding out her phone. She must've just finished her phone call. "I found what I was looking for," I said, slipping past her and heading back outside before she could stop me.

I climbed into my car and pulled away from the curb quickly. I could feel the book burning against my back. The notations didn't make much sense to me, but if it was some kind of blackmail log, then it had to hold the key to the identity of Bethany's murderer. This was exactly the kind of clue I was looking for.

20

"What are you smiling at?" Tracy looked at me sideways as she came up to the front desk, holding a stack of papers. She slid behind the front desk and began filing the papers into the cubby holes we kept back here.

I'd been staring out into the front lobby as I sorted the mail, probably with a dreamy look on my face.

After I had found that ledger in Bethany's office, I'd gone right to Detective Patel. This was the kind of hard evidence I needed to show her to help find Bethany's killer.

"Explain yourself," Patel had said, after leafing through the pages. I took her through finding it in Bethany's office— emphasizing the fact that Angeline had let me inside, that I hadn't broken in—and bringing it straight to her.

Patel had sighed, then called for an officer. She'd told him to put the ledger into evidence and not let anyone else touch it. Then she'd brought me to Chief Tate and had me tell him what I'd found.

"I have to admit, you did good here," Tate had said,

gesturing towards the ledger that was being carried away by an officer. "Now you need to let us do our job."

I had given them assurances that I would stay out of it and had hurried back to the inn, a smile plastered across my face.

We were one step closer to finding Bethany's killer, which meant Tony Vasco was bound to reconsider and make another offer on the inn. Who knew all this would happen when I agreed to come to Washington? For the first time all week, I was looking forward to returning home to California.

Now it seemed like the smile hadn't gone away. I turned towards Tracy and kept my tone neutral. "Nothing much. Just about how crazy everything has been. I hope the police are getting closer to finding Bethany's killer so things can settle down. Any word on the charity auction?"

Tracy shrugged. "The board of directors has been tight-lipped about it around me. I think they're still trying to figure out what to do with Bethany gone. She really ran that place, but I know they don't want to disappoint the Children's Art Studio."

"Well, I hope they figure it out soon. It sounds like a great event, really valuable for the community. I'd hate to see it canceled this year."

"Not in our control, but I agree. I need to stop by their office and check in with them again soon."

Lola trotted over from behind the desk, and I ruffled her ears as she passed. She sat in front of Tracy, who glanced at me, then also gave some affection to the dog. I hid my smile as she did. I guess it wasn't so easy to hide that soft side, after all. Lola, finished with her pats, went back to her spot behind the desk.

Across the lobby, in the bistro, people were laughing and

eating and having a good time. It finally felt like things were coming together.

Now that the police had real evidence of Bethany's blackmailing schemes, they were that much closer to finding her killer. And maybe I could still convince Tony Vasco to buy the inn. If only he could see how happy everyone was here right now.

"I think Lola needs to go outside," Tracy said, putting down the envelopes she'd been sorting through. She led Lola away into the courtyard, a poop bag sticking out of her pocket. With a quick flash of her hand, she snuck Lola a treat as they walked away.

Without giving myself a chance to question what I was about to do, I whipped out my phone and dialed a number.

"Mr. Vasco? This is Simone Evans. I was wondering if you could come by the Hemlock Inn this afternoon."

Twenty minutes later, I was leading Tony Vasco through the halls of the inn. He'd been hesitant on the phone, unsure that the police were, in fact, close to finding Bethany's killer, but I'd promised him he wouldn't regret coming out. Now all I had to do was convince him that I was right.

"Each room is decorated with a unique style," I explained as we walked, pointing out different rooms as we passed them. "My aunt had a quirky style, and it's reflected in her design choices for the room."

"Yes, I've seen a couple of them," Vasco said, his hands clasped behind his back. "Not my cup of tea, exactly, but it shouldn't be hard to correct."

"Correct? What do you mean?" We'd entered the lobby at this point, having finished our circuit of the rooms. I led him towards the bistro next.

"All my B&Bs have the same mid-century modern style,"

he explained. "It takes some effort to work out the quirks of the establishments I buy, but I get rave reviews from all the guests who stay in them. It's a tried and true design."

I smiled and nodded, ignoring the tightening in my stomach. This guy would get rid of all the quirks that made the Hemlock Inn special? Maybe I could talk him into leaving a few things intact.

"What are you doing here?" Nadia's raised voice carried over from the front desk, and Vasco and I stopped and looked in her direction. Chief Tate, Detective Patel, and a few cops in uniform were at the front desk.

"Chief Tate, what are you doing here?" I took a step in his direction.

"We're looking for Tracy Williams," Tate said, looking around the lobby.

"She's in the courtyard," Nadia said.

"What's this all about?" I asked.

Tate motioned to the uniformed officers behind him, communicating with his eyes, and they headed off in the courtyard's direction. I turned back to Tate and Detective Patel.

"What's going on?" I asked, my gaze darting between the two of them.

"Ms. Evans, we're going to need you to stay behind the desk," Tate said, holding a hand out to keep me back. I looked to Detective Patel, who had a grim look on her face.

"What's going on?" I demanded.

"This is outrageous!" Eddy's voice came from the courtyard. I hadn't even realized he'd gone back there.

I whirled around in time to see the two uniformed officers walking out of the courtyard, Tracy between the two of them. Her eyes were wide and scared, and she locked gazes with me.

As they led her past, I struggled to understand what was going on. Lola ran out of the courtyard after them, barking, but Eddy grabbed her as she went by and held her back.

"I'm sorry, Simone," said Detective Patel, but she didn't look upset about what was happening. "We're arresting Tracy for the murder of Bethany Stevens."

∽

THE COPS WOULDN'T SHARE MUCH ELSE with us. They left us standing in the lobby, gaping through the double doors while they loaded Tracy into the back of a cruiser.

"I think I had better get going," Tony Vasco said. I'd forgotten he was still here.

"I'm so sorry about that. There must be some kind of mistake." I looked around, trying to think of some way to save this. "Are you sure you don't want to look at the bistro?"

His smile was tight and small. "I think it's best if I leave now. You clearly have a lot to take care of." He left without another word, leaving me to stare after him.

"How could they think Tracy killed Bethany?" Eddy asked. I jumped; I hadn't heard him walk up.

"I don't know. She hated Bethany, didn't she?" I thought about that blackmail log I'd found. Had something in there pointed to Tracy?

"Hated doesn't mean murderer," Eddy said. "Should we get her a lawyer or something?"

"Probably. I'll call Ron and see if you can help. You go back to the bistro."

Eddy left me in the lobby, Nadia behind the front desk with wide eyes. The lobby was quiet after so much turmoil. I pulled out my phone and sent Ron a text letting him know what had happened. I was too flustered to get on the phone with him, but I knew he'd do what he could to help Tracy.

What was going to happen now? Was Tracy a killer? Or were the police looking in the wrong direction? Would Tony Vasco buy the inn with the general manager suspected of murder? Or would he consider this something else not part of his "image" and run as fast as he could? I needed to talk to him again, and soon.

For now, all I could do was try to take care of the inn. Sylvia had left it to me, and, with Tracy gone, I was in charge. Could we get through this in one piece?

21

T he next morning, I woke early for a run. I'd been up late, checking with Ron to make sure Tracy got legal representation and keeping an eye on the inn staff, but once I'd gone to bed, I'd slept like a log.

My shoes smacked against the road as I ran, the only sound accompanying me on this run. A couple birds chirped, but no cars passed me, and I was left alone with my thoughts.

Was Tracy a murderer? Had my aunt trusted a murderer? Tracy was rude and grumpy, but that didn't make her a killer. But the police wouldn't have arrested her without solid evidence, right? I barely knew the woman; maybe she was a killer.

The woods loomed from behind the inn as I approached, finished with my run. The woods looked much darker and gloomier today than they had on previous days. Was that only because the weather was turning, getting colder and stormier as the season progressed? Or could the trees feel Tracy's absence? Were they sad about her arrest?

I showered when I got back from my run, and Lola and I headed downstairs together. The run had given me some energy, but I was still anxious after Tracy's arrest last night and concerned about the future of the inn. Nadia was standing at the front desk, staring down at her hands.

"Hey, how are you doing?" I asked, approaching the front desk.

Nadia glanced up, her cheeks streaked with tears. "What are you doing here?"

I paused a foot away from the desk, confused. "I wanted to see how you're doing. I know last night was probably pretty intense. Do you need help checking in guests?"

"I thought you were looking for Bethany's killer. And you just let them take Tracy away last night!"

I held up my hands in an attempt to placate her. "I'm not sure what you mean, but the police wouldn't have arrested Tracy if they didn't have evidence that she was involved."

"Oh, please, Tracy would never hurt a fly. In fact, she made me carry spiders out of here all the time. It was really gross."

I walked up to the desk, putting my hands down between us. "I don't know what you'd have me do. The police have evidence. Ron is getting her a lawyer. It's all being taken care of."

"You have to help her! She didn't do this!" Nadia's voice had turned to a wail, and I hurried over to her side of the desk and pulled her into a hug.

Nadia calmed down after a few moments, and I passed her a tissue.

"Tracy's not a killer. She didn't do this. You have to help her." Her voice was steady, though I could hear the pain behind the words.

"I'll give Ron a call and see what I can do to help. Now, what can I do to help you here? There must be things Tracy normally does at the inn that you need help with now."

She crossed her arms, her eyes turning hard. "Find the real killer. That's what you can do to help me."

Nadia wouldn't say any more, so I left her at the front desk and went into the bistro. The silence hit me like a wall. Normally bustling at this hour, the bistro was eerily silent. Had people heard about Tracy's arrest and stayed away?

Eddy was wiping down a table and glanced up when I entered. He hurried over to me and pulled me into a hug.

"I still can't believe it," he said, pressing his full weight onto mine. I struggled to stay standing.

"We'll figure it out, don't worry," I said, patting his back awkwardly.

He pulled away suddenly, gripping my shoulders in his hands. "You're going to save her, aren't you?"

"Save who?"

"Tracy, of course! She didn't kill anyone! I've been thinking about it all night, and it's ridiculous that the police think she did it. She's no killer. But this inn needs her if we're to survive."

I studied his earnest, open face, his emotion surprising me. The staff at the Hemlock were loyal, that was for sure. But were they right? Had the police arrested the wrong person?

"All I'm trying to do right now is get some coffee," I said finally. "Do you need any help out here, or can I go look for some?"

Eddy shook his head and stepped to the side, so I moved past him to get to the kitchen. Pierre, at least, should have something caffeinated for me.

"No, I am sorry, we are all out," he said, crossing his arms over his chest. My eyes flew between him and Hank, who'd left the sink to come greet me.

"What do you mean you're all out?" I asked, cringing at the hint of hysteria in my voice. "How can you be out of coffee?"

Pierre sighed. "I am sorry. One of our orders was incorrect, and they did not bring enough of the coffee with the last shipment. I have requested a speedy replacement, but nothing in this town moves fast."

From the exasperation I could hear in his voice, it sounded like Pierre had dealt with slow orders in Pine Brook before. How did we compare with his hometown in France?

I hung my head, feeling the exhaustion coursing through me. I really needed some coffee, but an incorrect order was a big deal, and it was probably something Tracy would normally deal with. I didn't have a lot of options at this point.

"All right, I'll start researching new coffee vendors," I said, looking up. "Maybe I can find someone new we can start working with. If anyone needs anything else from me, I'll be in town."

Fifteen minutes later, I was standing in line at Cuppa Joe's, wringing my hands and praying they still had coffee in stock. I'd jolted awake instantly when I entered the shop and sniffed the beans in the air, and soon I was clutching my cup, gulping down the coffee like I'd stumbled on a fountain in the desert.

I'd also found a few coffee vendors online with my phone and put in requests for quotes. Maybe if our current vendor knew we were looking elsewhere, they'd get their act together and deliver the right orders.

Feeling refreshed, I stepped outside, my thoughts turning back to Tracy. Nadia and Eddy were convinced she was innocent. Were they right? Or was Tracy fooling everyone? She was grouchy, yes, but that didn't make her a killer.

If the police kept her in jail for long, Tony Vasco might not buy the inn, and I didn't know what I was going to do if that happened. I couldn't run this place on my own.

"Watch out!" someone yelped.

I was jolted out of my thoughts as I crashed into someone on the sidewalk. I kept my grip tight on my coffee cup and took a couple steps back.

"Sorry about that," I said, getting my bearings.

Victor Stevens stood in front of me, gripping his own cup of coffee and looking annoyed at the collision.

"It's okay," he said, softening once he saw it was me. "I didn't see you there. My mind has been elsewhere these days."

"Did you hear about Tracy?" I asked, assuming he was relieved the police had arrested someone for the murder of his wife.

He nodded. "I still can't really believe it. I know I should probably be angry, but it's so sad. Tracy seemed like such a good person, but I guess she was hiding something much darker. She and Bethany never got along. I'd always assumed their animosity towards each other didn't have any real backbone to it. They would argue, but it could seem half-hearted. But I guess Tracy felt more strongly about it than I realized."

"Did you tell the police all this?"

"I did. I'm not sure if it helped anything. I get the sense they found some evidence that pointed to Tracy."

The blackmail log flashed in front of my eyes. Was Tracy on the list of people Bethany had been blackmailing? Had I handed the police all the evidence they needed to arrest her?

"Well, I should get going," Victor said, breaking the silence.

"Heading into the office?" I asked. It was almost ten a.m. Why wasn't he in the office already?

To my surprise, he tensed up at the question and sputtered out an answer. "I... no, I was... going to meet someone," he said finally, looking around us as if hoping that person would show up and save him from me. "A few meetings this morning, some things to take care of, you know how it goes, I'm sure?"

I nodded along like I had any idea about what he was talking about. Why was he so jumpy? Was he lying about what he was doing?

"You must be so relieved they've arrested someone for your wife's murder." I paused, gnawing at my bottom lip. "But do you think they've arrested the right person?"

"Why would you question that? You don't think Tracy killed her?" He looked at me sideways.

"Well, I'm not so sure. Yes, they didn't like each other, but dislike doesn't necessarily lead to murder." I watched him closely, trying to see any reaction to my suggestions.

He kept his face still. "I don't know what would drive a person to kill someone else. I think we should let the police handle all of this."

"You're right, I'm sorry. It must be so exhausting having to answer all the questions from the police while you're trying to grieve. I don't mean to make you think about it more now."

"That's all right. And yes, it is exhausting." Victor mopped his forehead with a handkerchief.

"I bet. Detective Patel spoke to me a second time and it's very intimidating, you know. Did they interview you a second time?"

"They did. I didn't have much to share. And now, with Tracy arrested, it looks like the investigation is over." His voice was neutral, but he wouldn't meet my gaze. Was he hiding something?

"You must really miss Bethany since it was just the two of you at home."

"Yes, it's so quiet in the house without her," he said with a sigh. "But I'm trying to keep myself busy with work."

"Like you did the night she was murdered?"

"Yes." He side-eyed me again.

"Good thing you probably had cameras in your office building to back that up, right? To prove you weren't the one who killed her?" I blurted.

"What are you getting at, Ms. Evans? Are you accusing me of something?"

"I'm not accusing you of anything. I'm just asking questions. I want to get to the truth."

His eyes widened and his face turned a shade of red I wasn't expecting. He grabbed my arm and gave me a shake, his grip tight.

"And the truth is, Tracy murdered my wife and that is final." His eyes darted around again, his voice low and menacing. "Where I was that night is none of your damn business. What my wife did in her personal time is none of your damn business. Our marriage is none of your damn business." He glowered at me for a moment longer, then stalked away.

I rubbed my arm where he had grabbed me. Where had that anger come from? He'd been so kind when we first met.

He was like a different person now. Was it because I'd asked where he was the night his wife was murdered or was it something else? Was Victor a grieving husband, or had the police arrested the wrong person?

22

I finished my coffee and headed back to the inn. I'd gotten a couple responses from coffee vendors, so I thought I'd go back and look through the different quotes. I also wanted to think about Victor some more. Had I judged him wrong at first? Was there a killer under the calm surface?

Back at the inn, my thoughts drifted to the charity auction. Camille had said we would work together on this event, but I hadn't heard from her in days. Did she know what had happened with Tracy? I found her number in Sylvia's office, with the rest of the paperwork for the charity auction, and gave her a call.

"Yes, yes, I heard all about the arrest," Camille said after I explained why I was calling. "Such a shame, but it shouldn't affect us too much. I'm working on gathering some more items for the event, but we're lucky. Bethany did a lot of the work before she passed away. I can stop by later to go over the remaining details if you'd like to help."

"That would be great," I said, relieved. Finally, something I could do to feel like I was helping.

"Wonderful. I'm about to step into a meeting, but I'll call you soon to set something up. Don't worry, we'll figure this all out."

She said goodbye, and we hung up, leaving me feeling more confident than I had felt all day. If we could at least figure out this event, that was one thing I could do to not ruin my aunt's reputation.

I went into the bistro to see if I could help out. A few more people had shown up since that morning, though it was definitely quieter than it usually was at this time of day. I tried to keep uneasiness from creeping up my spine about what the quiet meant and stopped by Estelle and Miles' table.

"Ah, Simone, we were just talking about you," Estelle greeted me. "So dreadful to hear about Tracy. How are you doing with everything?"

I shrugged. "I'm doing okay. I haven't heard anything from Ron about her, but I'm trying to keep things running here."

"Well, if you need anything, let us know," Miles said, his expression sad. "We love this place, we love Tracy, and we loved your aunt. We'd hate to see anything happen to the Hemlock Inn. Where else would we go for delicious scones?"

I smiled down at his plate, pleased to see they were enjoying the chef's new recipe. Pierre had been a little nervous about trying something new, but as I looked around the rest of the bistro, I noticed several guests were happily eating the newest item on the menu.

I'd wanted to feel like I'd contributed something to the inn, and scones had always been my favorite pastry. Pierre had been a little resistant at first, but the scones were a hit.

"I'm so pleased you like them," I said. "Pierre put a lot of effort into coming up with the recipe."

"They are marvelous," Estelle said. "Now, how are things going with our investigation? How are we going to save Tracy?"

I raised my eyebrows and looked between the two of them. "What do you mean, save?"

"You don't believe she did it, do you?" Estelle asked, pressing her hand against her chest. "Tracy would never!"

"I know she can be a bit prickly, but she's not a killer," Miles said. "Your aunt was a good judge of character, and she trusted Tracy with everything here. We don't believe for one second that she did this."

I sighed. They were just like Nadia and Eddy, convinced that Tracy was innocent. Was it possible all of them were right? They knew Tracy better than I did; was there another side to her I hadn't seen yet?

"Something weird did happen with Victor earlier today," I said slowly, still feeling his grip on my arm. I told them about his outburst. "I did basically accuse him of murder, but he was so angry. Maybe he did hurt his wife?"

"If you ask me," Estelle said, dropping her voice down, "I never trusted that Victor. He always seemed a bit too fake to be real. I'm not surprised he has a violent side."

It was clear Victor was hiding something; the question was, was he hiding a guilty conscience, or something more sinister?

A loud commotion coming from the kitchen interrupted my thoughts. I hurried back there, waving goodbye to Miles and Estelle. What could possibly go wrong now?

"It's not as bad as it seems," Hank said, standing at the door of the kitchen and wringing a hand towel. I moved around him and took in the scene.

One of the industrial sinks in the back was spewing water from the faucet, straight up into the ceiling. Javier hurried about, trying to mop up the water as it rained down from the sky. Penny and Eddy stuck their heads into the kitchen and both cringed at the mess.

"This is ridiculous!" Pierre tossed down his hand cloth and was staring at the sink, as Javier milled about trying to fix it. He looked around the room and rushed over to me when he saw me enter.

"You! You must do something about this!" he said, waving his hands in the air and pointing at me, his French accent coming out strong. I looked from him to the sink and back again, remembering something similar that had happened at Antonio's once.

I rushed over to the sink and crouched down, water splashing onto my back. Reaching under the sink, I found the main water valve and shut it off. The water shooting out of the sink sputtered, then stopped, and the room was silent.

"Does anyone have the number of a plumber we can call?" I asked, turning back to the staff. "We'll need someone to fix the pipe if we want to use the sink again."

"This is ridiculous!" Pierre said again, his French accent coming out much stronger.

"Pierre, it's all right," I said, putting up my hands and aiming for a soothing tone. "We can get someone in here to deal with this. I'm sure someone in town can repair the sink."

"It is not just that! It is everything! Murders and arrests and guests sending their food back! I cannot do this anymore!"

"What do you mean?" I implored.

He sighed, his eyes weary and sad. "I loved Sylvia, and I

loved working for her, but I cannot work here anymore. Not with everything that has been going on. I am sorry, but I quit."

"Wait, you can't leave!" I pleaded, following him to the back of the kitchen, where he collected his things. Who would cook the dinner tonight? I couldn't let him leave like this, not with everything already a mess. You can't run a bistro if you don't have a cook!

"Pierre, please, let's try to work this out," I said, looking around the kitchen, as if the answer to my chef quitting was hidden in the pots and pans.

"I am sorry." He pulled on a cap and wrapped his jacket around his shoulders. "I wish you all the best, and I hope they release Tracy soon. She is a good person." He squeezed my arm and walked out the back door, his shoulders hunched against the wind.

I turned around slowly, facing the kitchen staff. "What are we going to do now?" I asked, seeing only averted eyes and crestfallen faces.

Eddy rang the tiny bell to indicate that there were more orders to be made, but how were we going to cook without a cook in the kitchen?

"I can step in." Hank spoke up, his face as red as his hair. I don't think he'd ever spoken up in this kitchen before.

I narrowed my eyes at him, remembering the fiasco with the wine glasses the day before. I was desperate, but was I this desperate? What would Sylvia think if I let Hank help? She wasn't here anymore, but her opinion still mattered.

"I can do it." Hank hurried up to me, probably reading the hesitation on my face. "I know I've had some screw-ups." That was an understatement! I held in a scoff. "But I can do this. I've always wanted the chef job here, but Pierre was so good, I didn't think I'd have the chance..."

Hank trailed off, averting his eyes from mine. He glanced up once, saw that I was still looking at him, and tried again. "Give me a chance, Simone, please. A trial run! I know someone who can come in and fix the sink, and I can get Javier to help with serving, and we can make it work!"

Javier had gone back to his respective corner, not interested in the outcome of this discussion, and instead focused on getting out the rest of the orders for the night. Penny and Eddy were out front to help with the rest of the guests. Hank was the only one still here.

Hank's expression was so earnest, I could feel my defenses wavering. Yes, he'd had some mishaps since he'd been at the inn, but everyone deserved a second chance, right? I wished I'd gotten another chance after punching that idiot at Antonio's bar. Plus, it wasn't like I had a better option right now.

"All right," I said with a nod. "You can try tonight. If it goes well, we'll see about bringing you on full-time. Now, what can I do to help?"

Hank's face lit up. "I've got to get some things ready for dinner and call a plumber. Why don't you take those drinks out to the guests?" He motioned to a tray of drinks sitting on the counter.

I smirked when I saw the cocktails. Ah, yes, back where I started, serving drinks. I lifted up the tray and pushed my way back through the swinging doors into the dining room. Someone had written down on a napkin which tables the drinks were for, so I quickly passed them out. A couple of people asked for refills, so I got to work on filling orders.

Would Hank live up to Pierre's high standards? If Hank did poorly in the kitchen, would guests even keep coming back? The bistro made up a sizable portion of the inn's revenue, and it wasn't only guests of the inn who came to eat here.

A scan of the dining room as I dropped off drink orders confirmed that the number of town residents eating here outweighed the number of inn guests. If we couldn't make this new setup work, the bistro, and the inn, might fail.

23

After finishing up on the open drink orders, I left Hank in charge in the kitchen and went back to the front desk. We'd gotten a delivery of towels that needed folding before they could go into guest rooms, so I got to work.

A tall woman approached the front desk, looking very stylish and somewhat out of place in the rustic inn. Her blond hair was cut short, with fringe bangs, and her blue eyes shined bright.

"Hi," she said, smiling. "My name is Francine. I'm looking for Angeline."

"Welcome," I said. "I'm afraid Angeline isn't here right now. Can I help you with something?" This was strange. Was Angeline telling people they could find her at the inn? Didn't she have an office she and Bethany had worked out of? I tried not to let my confusion show on my face.

"Oh shoot," Francine said, looking chagrined. "She left a message saying she would be here. I guess she said she was stopping by for something. Have you seen her at all today?"

I shook my head, remembering what Nadia had said when I'd shown up. No one but guests had been by all day. "No, she hasn't been by today. I haven't spoken to her in a couple of days either. Was there something you needed? I'm helping with the charity auction, so if it's related to that, I might be able to assist."

At those words, Francine's cheeks reddened, and my eyebrows raised at the sight. Why would bringing up the charity auction cause her to react that way?

"No, I'm not here about the auction," she said. "I shouldn't be telling you this, but I need to find Angeline because I'm one of her new clients. We planned to meet to go over our contract, but I can't seem to find her anywhere. My lawyer had a bunch of questions, and I wanted to get them cleared up." She waved a stack of papers in the air.

"One of her new clients? I thought Angeline worked for Bethany?"

"Well, she did. But she's been starting this online art gallery, and I'm going to help her get more clients. We met through Bethany, actually. I think she was planning on leaving Bethany soon, but then she got murdered. Such a shame." Francine shook her head sadly.

"Wait, so you're saying Angeline was using Bethany's connections to start an art gallery? Did Bethany know about this?"

"I doubt it. I know I'd be mad if my assistant was poaching my friends."

"So she was trying to get other clients through Bethany, too?"

"I think she was. We didn't talk about her other clients, but I got the impression when she first came to me that I wasn't the first person she had asked." Francine brushed a lock of hair out of her face. "And she looked happy with herself, so I figured she was finding success, too. But I shouldn't talk about this," she added, glancing around the lobby again. "I mean, I know Bethany is dead, and so maybe it doesn't matter anymore, but I don't think Angeline would want this getting out."

I was still processing Francine's words. What had Angeline gotten herself into? She'd said so many positive things about Bethany when we'd first talked. In fact, she'd said so many that I had been a little suspicious about whether she was being honest.

Having spent even a little time with Bethany, I knew she wasn't a pleasant person, and when Angeline and I had first talked, her kind words had surprised me. I'd assumed that maybe Angeline had seen another side of Bethany that I hadn't experienced. But the more I learned about Bethany, the more she seemed like a nightmare to work with. Had Angeline decided she'd had enough and decided to leave?

"Well, if you hear from Angeline, will you please tell her I stopped by?" Francine said.

I nodded, still thinking about what she'd told me as she walked out of the inn. Did I believe Francine was telling the truth? There'd be no reason for her to lie. I picked up another towel and folded it.

If Angeline had lied about how she felt about Bethany and what she was planning on doing now that Bethany was gone, could I believe anything she'd said?

I remembered her alibi; were her parents lying for her? I didn't know what I could believe about what she had told me, and I wondered what this meant for Tracy.

If Angeline was lying about what she was up to, would that cast enough suspicion on her to get Tracy released from jail? I didn't know how that worked, but I knew I needed to get some answers from Angeline.

Unfortunately, she didn't pick up my phone call. What else could I do? I was out of my depth here and I needed help.

What would Sylvia do? She'd ask for help, no matter where she had to go to get it.

24

The next morning, I stood in front of the police station, anxiety coursing through me. Was this the right move? I was here already, and Ron had given me the information I needed. I couldn't leave. I squared my shoulders and walked into the building.

Twenty minutes later, I was sitting across from Tracy. She was still at the local jail while her lawyer and the D.A. discussed her situation. Officer Scott had been at the front desk when I entered the police station, and, after some begging on my part, he agreed to let me see Tracy.

We were in a large room with bars running down the middle. On one side, there was a table and chairs and a hallway that led to the rest of the police station. On the other side of the bars, sat Tracy.

The cell she was in was as large as the room, with a single window high in the far wall. There was a bunk bed with two mattresses, a small table with a single chair, and a toilet. We both kept our gaze away from the toilet. Officer Scott stood outside the room, waiting for me.

Tracy's dreads were pulled back into a low ponytail. Her

nose ring had been removed, and she looked tired, heavy bags hanging under her eyes. She was wearing a grey, long-sleeved t-shirt, grey pants that were too short, and white slip-on shoes.

She'd pulled the chair away from the table and set it in the middle of the cell so that she was facing me, and her hands were clasped in her lap. She picked at the skin on one of her fingernails.

"How are you?" My voice broke the silence, echoing in the cavernous room.

She shrugged. "Can't say it's my favorite place to be. My lawyer says it's better than county jail, at least. How did you get in here?"

I pointed over my shoulder with my thumb. "Officer Scott is right outside. When I told him it was hard to run the inn without my business partner, he agreed to give me five minutes with you. I told him I didn't know the password for the payroll system and I was worried I wouldn't be able to pay the staff."

"Better hope he doesn't hear you," she said, a half-smile ghosting her face.

I wasn't worried. It had been a weak lie, and I had a feeling Officer Scott had let me back here more out of compassion than anything else. We probably only had a few more minutes together, though.

"Have the police told you anything about the evidence they have against you?" I kept my voice low.

She narrowed her eyes. "I heard you found a spreadsheet in Bethany's ceiling that had my name on it. Care to comment?"

I winced. "I-I didn't realize your name was on it when I brought it to the police. I thought it would lead to her killer."

She snorted. "Yes, the police had the same idea. Unfortunately, they've gotten it into their heads that *I* am her killer."

"It doesn't make any sense. What reason would you have for killing her? Why was your name even on that spreadsheet? What did Bethany have on you?"

Her face closed up. "My lawyer says I shouldn't talk about it. He's trying to work with the D.A. to figure out how she wants to charge me, but he said to keep what we talk about to myself, *especially* in here."

My brow furrowed. "What do you mean, especially in here? What does he think would happen?"

She shrugged, nonchalant, but her eyes were hard. "Can't say for sure. All I know is, it's taking a while for evidence to get to the D.A. But once it does, my lawyer is confident I'll be cleared."

I sat back, mulling over her words. What evidence needed to get to the D.A.? They had the log already, right? Was there some other evidence that would prove Tracy hadn't done it? Why was it taking so long to get it to the D.A.?

"How's Lola doing?" Tracy's voice cut through my thoughts.

"She's all right. She misses you. We all miss you."

Tracy's eyes filled with tears, and she hung her head, taking a few breaths. When she looked back up, her eyes were dry.

"Thank you for coming by. Tell everyone at the inn I'm thinking about them." Her voice was controlled, robotic, like she was holding in her emotions.

I leaned forward, gripping the sides of the chair, emotion coming over me. "I know you didn't do this. You're only here because of what I found, but I can't believe my aunt would work with a murderer. The real killer is out there, and I'll find them. I promise you that."

Her eyes widened, but I turned away before she had a chance to say anything. I didn't want to make her talk if she didn't want to. Instead, I left the room, nodding to Officer Collins as I went.

I hadn't even realized that I felt so strongly about her innocence until I saw her sitting in that tiny room. The words of Nadia and Eddy and the Adlers had me questioning Tracy's guilt, and my gut told me she was innocent.

I stepped back into the main room of the station, where all the officers' desks were, and took a few deep breaths. Seeing Tracy had been harder than I'd expected. She'd looked so sad and defeated. Was her lawyer doing all he could to get her out of there?

"What are you doing here?" Patel stood in front of me, her arms crossed and eyes narrowed. I glanced over my shoulder, but Officer Scott had already gone back to the front desk.

I turned back to Patel, copying her arm crossing. "I was speaking to Tracy. Is that a crime?"

"Why would you want to talk to her?"

"We're business partners. I needed help with something."

Patel studied me, as if looking for the lie, then shrugged and turned away. "I'm assuming you know your way out," she called over her shoulder.

"Wait!" I touched her arm to stop her, then dropped my hand when she glared at me. "What evidence do you have against Tracy? That blackmail log I found? There were dozens of other names on there. What makes you think it was Tracy?"

"I can't talk about an active case."

I took a step closer to her, dropping my voice. "I think you don't have any evidence on her. I think you're keeping her here because you're desperate and need someone to pin this on. I bet you don't have any real evidence." I was grasping at straws, hoping something would stick.

"Tate calls the shots here, all right?" Patel hissed, her voice low. "He makes the decisions about what we bring to the D.A. and how much we share. The real question you should be asking is, what does he have against your friend that makes him so eager to keep her locked up?" She took a step away from me, raising her voice. "Please leave, Ms. Evans. This area is restricted from civilians."

I stepped around her and walked towards the exit, ignoring the looks from the other police officers at their desks. Once I was outside, I took in a few lungfuls of air, feeling the tension in my shoulders loosen. That was the last time I wanted to visit a police station.

I got into my car and drove to the inn. What had Patel meant about Tate calling the shots? Did this secret history with Tracy explain why she was still sitting in the jail and why the D.A. didn't have the evidence she needed? Could he even do that?

I had to get Tracy out of there before it was too late and Tate shipped her off to county jail.

25

T he front desk was quiet when I arrived back at the inn, and Nadia asked me to monitor things while she finished cleaning up some rooms. I found my thoughts drifting as I stood there, images of Tracy sitting in jail floating through my mind.

A woman entered the inn, looking around frantically. "Has anyone seen Angeline?" she called out, and I waved her down. I recognized her as one of the committee members for the charity auction. Finally, someone who could help me figure out how planning the event was going.

"Hi Patrice, I'm Simone," I said, walking up to her with my hand outstretched. "What can I help you with?"

"Oh thank goodness," she said, squeezing my hand. "Someone to help. Everything is going wrong!"

I led her to the side, studying her as we went. It was clear she wasn't used to dealing with problems, and I was certain that Bethany's death had caused a lot of problems for her.

"Why don't you start at the beginning? What's going on?" I'd just spoken on the phone with Camille, and she'd said she had a handle on everything. So why was Patrice acting like everything was going wrong?

"We're completely behind schedule, and I can't find anyone to help!" Patrice looked about ready to burst into tears.

"Have you spoken to Camille or Angeline?"

"They are nowhere to be found!"

"Why don't you tell me what the issue is, and I'll see if I can help?" I offered.

Patrice nodded and pulled out a tablet. She walked me through the decisions that still needed to be made, mostly place settings and centerpieces. It did not seem as life or death as she had initially made it out to be, but I didn't want to question her hysteria.

Instead, I made some quick decisions, remembering that I was the only person here who could help. If Camille or Tracy ended up hating my decisions, well, then too bad for them.

I chose clear vases for the center of the tables, with bouquets of fresh-cut marigolds in each vase. Patrice had art drawings from the kids at the art center that we planned to display on place card holders and nestle amongst the flowers. Each place setting had a gold design, with floral accents surrounding the entire table.

Selecting designs from Patrice's samples made me even more excited about the charity auction. I hoped Tracy would be out of jail and we'd find Bethany's killer before the event started. I didn't know if I could do all of this otherwise.

"Thank you so much," Patrice said once we finished. "I really thought that was going to be much harder. See you at the event!" She gave me a wave and flounced away.

What was up with this organization and difficult to work

with women? It had felt good to make decisions about something like I had some control. Maybe I could do this after all.

The front desk was still quiet, and we didn't have any guests checking in soon, so I decided to check on Hank. Without Tracy here, someone had to be responsible for what was happening at the inn.

Penny was wiping down a table in the bistro when I entered.

"How are things going in here?" I asked.

"Not bad," she said. "Hank is really enjoying his new role. Plus, we've definitely had fewer accidents since you made him chef."

"Any number of accidents seems bad to me."

Penny laughed. "Don't worry, he's figuring it out. Being in control has given him more confidence. And the guests seem to really like his cooking."

Peering over tables, it did look like the guests were enjoying the food. But how were things coming along in the kitchen itself?

Things were more chaotic in the kitchen than when Pierre was in charge, but Hank seemed to have a handle on things. Javier was putting the food on plates and getting them sent out to the tables quickly.

"Are you sure you've got everything under control?" I asked.

"Of course," Hank said, waving his hand flippantly. He knocked down a stack of plates, and Eddy ran over to deal with the mess. Hank blushed and took a few steps to the side. "Well, not perfectly. But we're doing what we can."

He was right; food was being served and guests were happy and fed. Maybe agreeing to have him take over as chef hadn't been a bad idea after all?

Nick burst through the swinging doors, this time carrying a burlap sack. He smiled at me and waved hello, then walked over to Hank, lugging the sack behind him.

"All right, chef, where do you want them?" he asked Hank.

Hank's face lit up and he left his spot stirring something on the stove. I opened my mouth to say something, but Eddy spotted the pot first and hurried over to turn down the heat on whatever Hank was making before he set the place on fire.

Nick and Hank lifted the burlap sack onto the counter, and Hank shoved his head into the depths of the sack. With a chuckle, I moved closer to see what they were looking at.

Hank popped his head out, gripping two brown potatoes in hand. "They're perfect!" he said to Nick, holding them out reverently.

I shook my head with a snort at his awe, then saw the same look on Nick's face, and my eyes narrowed. Clearly I wasn't seeing something here.

"What's so special about a couple potatoes?" I asked, moving over so I was standing closer to the bag and peering inside.

"Potatoes are mother nature's greatest creation," Nick said, taking the two potatoes Hank was holding and placing them carefully back into the bag. "Full of fiber, potassium, and you can cook them a hundred different ways. A true chef knows the value of a good potato." He smiled up at Hank, who blushed at the compliment.

I couldn't resist grinning back at the two of them. I sure had stumbled onto a strange community at the Hemlock Inn, but I was enjoying many parts of it.

I left them to deal with the broken plates and glorious potatoes and went out to the bistro. Estelle and Miles were sitting at a table, and Estelle discreetly waved me over. I smiled and walked over to their table.

"Any news? How's Tracy?" Estelle asked once I was close enough for her to whisper.

"I went to see her earlier. She's doing okay. You were right; I don't think she killed Bethany." I leaned in close and lowered my voice. "Patel let it slip that Tate is keeping her there on purpose. I guess he's not handing over all the evidence to the D.A. She thinks he might have something against her."

"That rat," Estelle snapped. "What gives him the right? Anyone who knows Tracy would know she had nothing to do with that awful woman's death."

"I hope we can still put on this event," Miles said. "Tracy cares so much about the children's art gallery and, even though she's not here, I know she'd want us to keep moving forward with it."

I agreed. I wanted to do whatever I could to help with the event. I went back to the front desk, my thoughts spinning.

"You still haven't heard from her?" Patrice was back, still concerned.

"Who?" I asked, wondering why she was asking about Tracy.

"Angeline, of course." Ah yes, that made more sense. "I haven't heard from her all day and she's normally so responsive."

"Maybe she's dealing with some other things right now," I said, flipping through the mail that had arrived at the front desk while I was gone.

"I don't know." Patrice chewed on her bottom lip. "This isn't like her. She's normally the one calling all of us about these last-minute details. Where could she be? I hope nothing has happened to her." She left then, still upset about Angeline but without a clue of how to find her.

I filed the mail into the different cubbyholes, thinking about what she had said. Why wasn't Angeline answering her phone? Had something happened to her, or was Patrice overreacting? It did seem like a bad idea to go radio silent when we so desperately needed her help with the charity auction.

I sighed and looked at my watch. I still had some time to go look for her. I left a note at the front desk and headed out to my car. I'd be quick about it and get this figured out as soon as I could.

26

I pulled up in front of the single-story house and switched off the engine. Glancing at the address I'd found in Sylvia's office, I confirmed I was at the right place.

It felt odd to show up to Angeline's home like this, but after Patrice's visit and not hearing from Camille, it was clear I needed some help with the charity auction. Hopefully, Angeline would answer the door and help me figure out what to do.

I climbed out of my car and wrapped my jacket tighter around myself. The temperature had dropped a few degrees as the sun was setting, with rainclouds scuttling in. I hoped this wouldn't take long. I wanted to curl up with a good book and a mug of tea back at the inn, ready to put the day behind me.

The front yard was in disarray, and the porch sagged under my weight. A car parked in the driveway implied Angeline was at home. I stayed light on my toes as I climbed up the porch steps and knocked on the front door. No doorbell in sight.

I found it hard to believe that the glamorous Angeline I'd met previously lived here, but I knew I'd gotten the address correct. Besides, I lived in an inn; who was I to judge?

I stood for a few moments, shifting my weight back and forth between my feet. No answer at the door. I knocked again. Still nothing. I leaned in towards the door and called out Angeline's name, listening for an answer. Nothing.

I pulled out my phone and dialed her number again, wondering if she was avoiding the door. I couldn't hear a phone ringing inside, but that didn't mean she wasn't there.

I stood back from the porch and looked left and right. Both of her neighbors' homes looked empty, and no one had come outside at my knocking. Pine Brook seemed like the kind of town where someone knocking on your neighbor's door would cause you to come outside, but that didn't seem to be the case here.

I leaned further to the right and saw a small pathway leading to the back of the house. Maybe Angeline would hear me from the back door instead.

The grass was overgrown back here, and I picked my way through the weeds. I didn't want to admit it, but I was getting nervous about the event. With Tracy in police custody, it was all becoming too much to plan and I needed some help. Angeline seemed like my best option at this point.

Her backyard was small, with a tiny porch and a few outdoor chairs. The wind picked up and whirled around some leaves that had fallen off an old oak tree. There was a door just off the porch, propped open. I took a few steps closer to it.

As concerned as I was about Angeline, a partially

opened door didn't give me the legal right to enter some-one's home. However, I was getting desperate with the charity auction and wanted to do whatever I could to get Angeline's help. If that meant entering her home without an invitation, then so be it. She'd probably yell at me, but then I could tell her to call Patrice and deal with her event.

The porch door led into a kitchen. I wrinkled my nose at the strange smell permeating the air. Maybe she'd left out some food. I called out her name but got no response, so I took a few more steps inside. It was much warmer inside than it was outside—she must have her heat on.

Dirty dishes were piled in the sink and stacks of paper littered a small table. Looked like Angeline didn't keep things too tidy at home.

As I walked towards the hallway, I noticed a piece of paper with some doodles on it on the kitchen table. *"Ange-line's Art Gallery"* was written across the back in various flourishes. Looked like she was trying out different styles for a logo. I flipped over the paper to find some names written on the other side. Francine's was right at the top. Were these other friends of Bethany's that Angeline was taking on as clients?

Did Bethany find out what Angeline was doing and confront her? According to Francine, Angeline was planning on leaving Bethany as soon as she could. I didn't think Bethany would want that to happen. Had Bethany attacked Angeline in anger and Angeline had stabbed her? Why were they at the inn so late?

I put the piece of paper back down. I'd considered taking it with me, but I wanted to get Angeline's side of things before I accused her of anything. I snapped a quick picture of it, so I'd have it in case it came up, then headed into the hallway, calling out Angeline's name again so I wouldn't startle her.

As I walked toward the living room, I noticed a faint smell in the air, though it was different from the rancid smell I'd picked up in the kitchen. I paused halfway down the hallway, sniffing the air.

Why did that fainter smell, which smelled more like flowers and... citrus? Why did it feel familiar? The rancid smell, the rotting fruit or something else, overpowered anything else, and I continued forward. I must've been smelling Angeline's perfume.

A sofa faced away from the kitchen, and Angeline was sitting on it. The hair on the back of her head looked wet and matted. The room was in complete disarray, with her purse dumped out on the floor.

"Oh, there you are," I said, hurrying around to her side. "Did you not hear me? I've been banging the door down."

I halted in front of her, my mouth going dry and my throat clenching. Angeline stared up at me with blank eyes, her mouth slack. She sat stiff straight, with no stab wounds or bullet holes. But I knew those eyes wouldn't blink again. Angeline hadn't heard me because she was dead.

I stumbled back a few steps as my lunch sped up my throat, rushing out of the room before I threw up all over the crime scene.

I SAT on Angeline's back porch, a blanket wrapped around my shoulders. The police had asked if I wanted to wait inside, where it was warm, but I'd preferred to brave the outdoor winds if it meant I didn't have to stay inside with her body anymore.

I couldn't get the look in her eyes out of my head. It didn't look all that dissimilar from Bethany's look when I'd seen her last. I shivered and pulled the blanket tighter around my shoulders. Two women, now dead. Had the same person killed them?

Officer Scott had taken command of the crime scene, and I heard him put in a call to Detective Patel and then request the medical examiner once again. I was told to wait while they secured the scene. Would I get in trouble for essentially breaking into Angeline's house? If you find a dead body, does it count as trespassing?

The messy room, all the books and drawers and things thrown on the floor, it all made me wonder if Angeline had interrupted a robbery. As I was leaving the living room, some cops said something similar. But her getting killed so close to Bethany's death seemed like too much of a coincidence.

It was clear Tracy didn't have anything to do with this since she was still in police custody. But did this have anything to do with Bethany's death? Had Angeline gotten too close to the truth?

I stood at the sound of footsteps and turned around.

"Hello, Ms. Evans." Officer Scott scratched the back of his head and looked like he wanted to be anywhere but here right now. You and me both, buddy.

"I've got a few questions, if you don't mind," he said, waving me back down to the porch and taking a seat next to me.

He took me through the typical questions: why I was here, why I'd come back to the backyard, if I'd seen or heard anything suspicious. I emphasized the fact that the back-door was wide open when I arrived.

"What do you think happened?" I asked when he'd paused to jot down notes.

He flicked his gaze up to me, then back down at his notepad, shifting in his seat. I had the strangest sensation that he was about to lie to me.

"We're still figuring it out. Detective Patel should be by soon. Looks like it might've been a robbery."

My eyebrows rose at this. "You must believe that Tracy didn't do this, right?"

"Yes, but we have no indication yet that this case is related to Mrs. Stevens' murder. I just need your statement. Detective Patel will be in touch if she has any follow-up questions."

We went through the rest of his list and I promised to stay in town and be reachable if they needed anything from me.

Angeline's death had to be connected to Bethany's; this town was too small to have this many murders in one week. Angeline must've gotten too close to the truth and someone had silenced her. But who had decided that? Victor? Or someone else?

Or was it possible that Angeline had, in fact, killed Bethany, but then she started blackmailing the same person Bethany did, and that person had killed Angeline?

The murders were so different—one committed at the inn, the other committed in someone's home and made to look like a robbery—so it was possible that they'd been committed by two different people. Was there someone else out there I hadn't even considered covering up their tracks?

At least I knew Angeline was trying to take Bethany's clients. I'd mentioned the list I'd found to the police, and they had seemed interested in that. Maybe there was something in their history that would point to the actual killer.

I'd come here hoping to get Angeline's help, but now it seemed like that wasn't possible at all. How were we going to put on this auction if everyone planning it kept dying? And now, with two deaths, was I safe in Pine Brook?

27

Back at the inn, I couldn't stop thinking about the upcoming charity auction. There was still a lot to do, and I didn't know where to start. With Tracy in jail and Angeline dead, it seemed like I was running out of help.

I had spoken with Camille the day before, and she'd seemed confident that we could get everything done, but that was before Angeline had been killed. Did she even know what happened? Would she want to cancel the event, given everything that had been going on? The only way to know for sure was to call her.

"Hey, Camille, it's Simone," I said into my phone when she picked up. "Did you hear about what happened with Angeline?"

"I did," she said. "So tragic. She was a good woman."

"What does this mean for the charity auction? I mean, two dead women so closely attached to the event. Can we even still put it on?" I asked. It felt weird to continue planning, knowing all the death that surrounded the event.

"Of course," Camille said, and I imagined her flapping her hand at me in the way she did when she thought the other person was being silly. She seemed pretty casual about Angeline's death, but Angeline wasn't her assistant. Maybe they didn't work together all that closely or know each other all that well.

"It's only a short week away, and fortunately, most of the planning is more or less done," she went on. "I'm taking care of some last-minute details. Did you still want me to come by and go over those with you? I'm sorry I haven't had a chance to since we last spoke, but things have been hectic, as I'm sure you know."

"No, no, that's completely fine. No need to apologize." My face flushed as I realized how unnecessary it was for me to question the planning of the event when we had just talked about how well things were going. Camille was the event planner here, not me, so why did I think I could tell her how to do her job?

"Listen, I've got to run, but I promise to stop by soon and go over those details. Don't worry, Simone, everything will work out perfectly."

We said our goodbyes and hung up, and I felt more reassured that everything was, in fact, going to be okay.

Before I could check on the dinner rush in the bistro, a man stepped up to the front desk with his gaze down. I didn't think we were expecting any guests, but maybe Nadia had taken down a reservation without putting it in the system.

This man had dark hair, cut short, with pale skin and dark eyes. He looked up at me and flinched away when we made eye contact.

"Hi there, can I help you? Checking in?" I asked, noting

the lack of bags in his possession. Maybe he was looking for the bistro and didn't know about the side entrance that most people used.

"Are you Simone?" His voice was deeper than I expected.

I nodded. "Yes, can I help you with something?"

He glanced nervously around again, as if there was someone following him.

"I heard you've been looking for me," he said, facing me fully. "Martin told me you stopped by."

This was the man seen arguing with Bethany before she died. This was Damian.

I TOOK A STEP BACK, wondering what Martin had told him about me. I was standing in the empty lobby, alone with a man I had suspicions had killed Bethany, and maybe even killed Angeline.

"Sorry, I don't mean to scare you," he said, holding up his hands. "I came as soon as I heard. I knew I needed to talk to you."

I studied him then, realizing that his eyes were actually kind. It didn't seem like he was upset with me or mad that I had been asking around about him. Instead, it looked like he wanted to tell me something. Lola had stood when he approached, her hackles raised, but she calmed down once she saw I wasn't freaking out anymore.

"Why don't we go somewhere private?" I suggested, leading him out into the courtyard. Lola trotted after us, wanting to keep an eye on me.

It wasn't completely private, but it was more private than

the front lobby, and it kept us in view of anyone in the inn. If he tried to hurt me, I wouldn't be far from help. He didn't look murderous, but what did I know?

"Why have you been asking about me?" Damian asked once we were settled in the courtyard.

Lola approached him slowly, her head down. When he reached out and scratched her ears, she melted under his touch and lay down with her head on his shoe, staring up at him with adoring eyes. So much for my guard dog.

I cleared my throat. "I heard you had an argument with Bethany Stevens a few days before she died. I wanted to know what the argument was about."

Damian dropped his gaze from mine, and, to my surprise, his eyes welled up with tears and his shoulders shook as he tried to hold the tears in. Shocked at this display of emotion, I patted his shoulder as he worked his way through whatever he was feeling.

"Sorry about that," he said, wiping his nose with the back of his arm and sitting forward. "I still can't believe it's true."

"What's true?" I asked.

"Bethany's dead," he said, as if I'd forgotten that I'd been the one to tell him that. "When I got back, Martin, my landlord, told me what happened. I still can't believe it. I talked to her days ago."

"Where have you been?" I asked. "The police want to talk to you."

"I've been out of town. Taking care of a few things back where I live."

I paused for a moment, unsure of how to phrase my next question. "I'm guessing you didn't kill her?"

He smiled sadly. "No. I wanted to come back to Pine

Brook full time and try to make a life here so I could spend more time with Bethany. But now that she's gone, I don't know what I'm going to do."

Wait, make a life here? "She was going to leave Victor for you?"

It was Damian's turn to look at me in surprise and confusion. "What? No, she wasn't leaving him for me." His eyes widened then, as something must've clicked for him inside his head. "You don't know, do you?"

"Know what?"

"Bethany and I weren't lovers," he said with a chuckle. "We were half-siblings."

I blinked at his words, my mind slowly processing them. That was not what I was expecting.

"My mom and her dad had a fling years ago," Damian went on. "My mom took me away, while Bethany was raised by her mom. Our dad was never heard from again. My mom passed away six months ago, and she told me about the sister I never knew before she went. I've spent the last six months looking for this sister and realized she was in Pine Brook about a week ago."

That was around the time that he'd been seen arguing with her in town. Had things turned sour between the two siblings?

"I showed up on her doorstep last Wednesday," Damian continued. "I probably would've reacted the same way she did if someone showed up like that, disrupting my life and wanting to be a part of it. She told me to leave, that she didn't want me around. We ran into each other at the town square a couple days later, and she was upset that I hadn't left yet. I didn't know how to explain it, but I wasn't ready to leave. I wanted to get to know her. With my mom gone, she was the only family I had left."

I nodded as he talked. I could understand the desire to want to get close to family, even if you didn't know them well, and I could also see why Bethany would be upset about someone showing up and wanting to be her brother. It would be a lot to handle.

Damian continued talking. "The day before she died, she showed up at my apartment to make amends and introduce me to Victor. It seemed like something had changed in her. She said something about wanting to accept all of her family. I was so ready to start this new life with her. I needed to take care of a few things at home, so I told her I would be back and left town that same day. Apparently, she was murdered that night." His eyes filled up with tears again and he looked down. "If I'd never left, if I'd stayed with her, she might still be alive."

"You can't know that," I said, squeezing his shoulder. "If you'd stayed and tried to help her, maybe you'd be gone too."

Damian nodded and took a few deep breaths. "When I got back and heard you were looking for me, I knew I needed to come talk to you. I don't know what you're trying to do here, but I appreciate that you're looking out for my sister. I'm so sad I didn't get to know her better."

This was all a lot to take in, and I couldn't even imagine the pain Damian was dealing with, knowing he was so close to creating a new family and having it taken away from him so suddenly.

"What are you going to do now?" I asked.

"Go to the police. I figure they should know that our fight didn't mean anything. Then I'm hoping to go meet Victor. I don't know if I'll scare him off, his dead wife's half-brother, but I'd like to meet him."

Damian left then, promising to keep in touch.

I sat back against the settee after he'd gone. With Damian's alibi, if it were true, there was no way he could've come back to the inn and killed Bethany. I'd reached another dead end and had no idea where to go from here.

28

The next day, I was on my hands and knees in front of the fireplace, poking up the chute.

When the fireplace wouldn't light the night before, I'd wanted to call a professional to come take a look, but Nadia had told me that Tracy had always dealt with it herself to save money.

So, I'd put on the rattiest clothes I could find and had taken a look at the situation, but all this had left me with was a sore back and covered in ash. My thoughts drifted back to the case.

Tracy was still locked up, and no one was telling me what was happening with her. Victor was still at the top of my suspect list after his outburst, but I had to admit my evidence was weak. Damian had been suspicious, but learning about his connection to Bethany, I crossed him off my list.

What about Estelle, or Camille, or Ron, or Eddy? I was surrounded by strangers in Pine Brook and, while I wanted to trust them, I had to remember that I didn't know much about them, and every single person in this town could harbor a reason to kill Bethany. I shouldn't let myself be distracted by how kind everyone was; that kindness could hide a killer.

I was running out of time and needed to find the killer, fast, before someone else got hurt. Unfortunately, I didn't know where to start.

Miles came into the inn at that moment, a newspaper folded up under his right arm and his hands stuck in his pockets. Lola's head perked up at his arrival and she dashed out from behind the desk and ran over to him. He smiled and knelt, patting her head and rubbing her ears.

"That's sweet," I said, climbing up from my knees and wiping my hands on my jeans.

Miles smiled up at me. "Lola and I are good friends. I bring biscuits for her," he added, slipping one out of his pocket and passing it to the beagle. "Don't tell anyone," he said with a wink. "Tracy already thinks she's spoiled too much."

I had a feeling Miles was one person I could cross off my suspect list. His gentle demeanor didn't seem murder-y to me.

"Your secret is safe with me," I said with a wink. "No Estelle today?" I asked, glancing around the lobby.

"Not today," Miles said. "She's got her book club. Just me and the local news." He tapped the newspaper under his arm.

"Anything in there about Angeline's killer?" I asked with a nod to the newspaper. "I could really use some help with this investigation."

"Actually, yes," Miles said, passing it over to me. "The police are saying she interrupted a robbery and was hit over the head."

I skimmed the article. Miles was right. Did that mean

Angeline's death didn't have anything to do with Bethany's? This wouldn't help Tracy get out of jail.

"It's such a shame," Miles said. "Angeline was a good person."

"Everything's gotten so messed up. I came here wanting to help, and now there's two dead bodies, and the inn's general manager is sitting in jail. Why did I think I could make a difference here?"

Miles studied me for a moment, cocking his head to the side and smiling. "Did you know your aunt was scared about running this place by herself after your uncle passed away? It's true—it was all she could talk about after his death. I think she was looking for anything to focus her attention on that wasn't the fact that her husband of so many years was now dead. Tracy was working here by that point, so it's not as if she would have had to do things alone, but Sylvia wasn't great about asking for help. Oh, we all wanted to help her. We all offered to do whatever we could. But she felt like this place was her responsibility, and if she didn't make it perfect right from the start, then what was the point of even trying?"

I shifted my weight between my feet. "I didn't know that about her. I honestly don't know much about her, besides what I knew from when we were kids. She and my mom were less close as we got older, and my sister and I never did a good job of keeping in touch with Sylvia. I always assumed she was stellar at this job, because that's the image I have of her from when I was younger. Running this place like a true pro, no problems, no mishaps."

Miles laughed loudly, causing me to jump. "Sorry," he said, holding up a hand apologetically. "It's just—the idea of this place not having any mishaps—is pretty funny to me. If there's one thing you can count on with the Hemlock Inn, it's mishaps."

Miles' face sobered up, and he took a step closer to the front desk. "I know things seem tough right now. But I think you're being too hard on yourself. Yes, two women are dead, and that is truly awful. But they aren't dead because of you. Sylvia had good instincts, in business and in life, and if she left you the inn, knowing all that it takes to run this place, then I have to believe that you were meant to come here."

Miles gave a half-smile and patted my hand, then headed back to the bistro. Lola trailed after him, eager for more biscuits. He snuck her one more before going into the bistro and I smiled.

Sometimes I forgot how well the people in this town knew my aunt and how much I could learn from them. The confidence they had in me blew me away. Yet, I couldn't help questioning whether they were right.

"Ms. Evans, I was wondering if we could speak for a few moments." Tony Vasco stood at the front desk, his hands in his pockets, a small smile on his face.

I gave a jolt at his presence. "Mr. Vasco. I didn't see you there."

"I apologize for scaring you." His smile didn't waver.

"It's okay. I guess my mind was somewhere else." Like searching for a killer.

"Could we speak somewhere privately? It'll just take a few minutes."

I looked around the lobby. "Well, I should really stay here and keep an eye on things... Actually, never mind. I'm sure it'll be fine for a few minutes."

I led him away from the front desk and into the courtyard, where we could have privacy. True, it wasn't great to leave the front desk empty, but with Tracy gone, I was now completely responsible for the Hemlock Inn. Tony Vasco was my best chance of selling, so if he wanted to talk, then we would talk.

We settled onto the outdoor settee, chatting about the weather and other inconsequential matters. Vasco's suit was dark green today, less casual than the suit I'd seen him wear last time. His nails were trimmed and well-groomed, his fingers long and graceful.

"I was sorry to hear about what happened with Tracy," he said after we'd run out of pleasantries. "I've only spoken with her a couple of times, but it's hard to believe what the police are saying about her. Do you have any idea what's happening with her?"

I shook my head. "They aren't telling anyone much. Ron was able to get her a lawyer and they're hoping she'll be released soon." I didn't mention that I'd gone to the town jail to see her. I was still processing everything she had shared with me.

"Well, I hope it all gets cleared up soon. I'm sure the police wouldn't arrest her if they didn't have good evidence, but I can imagine how tough this must be for you, having to manage the inn by yourself."

"Luckily, the staff here is great," I said with a warm smile, thinking about all the ways everyone had stepped up since Tracy was taken to jail. "It's made things easier for me."

"That's great to hear." Vasco smiled again, but it was tighter this time, and it didn't quite reach his eyes. "I wanted to speak with you today about the Hemlock. As you know, I made an offer to your aunt several weeks ago. At the time, she wasn't sure about selling. Apparently, she was rather sick and didn't want to make any decisions until she recovered, or didn't."

I nodded at his words, understanding what he wasn't saying. Ron had told me the same thing, that Sylvia hadn't wanted to accept an offer to sell if she didn't know for sure that she'd be around to deal with the outcome of the sale. Even then, she knew she might die, and she didn't want to leave Tracy to clean up her mess.

"When I made my initial offer, Sylvia was running this place like a pro," Vasco went on. "Guests were interested in staying here, and the bistro was packed all the time. It was quite a sight to behold. Now, however... Well, I don't need to tell you how things have changed. I'm sure you can see it all for yourself."

"Yes," I said carefully, unsure of what he was getting at. "It's true that business has slowed down recently. We've had some cancellations, and from what others have told me, fewer people are eating at the bistro. But I can assure you, this will pass. This inn is a great place to stay. You wouldn't regret your decision to buy it."

I didn't know if I believed any of what I was saying—how did I know if the inn could survive the decrease in guests?—but I only needed to convince Tony Vasco. It would've been easier to do this if I had Tracy beside me, as she knew all the ins and outs of this business. She would know if we should be worried about the cancellations. But Tracy wasn't here, so I had to save this place.

"Ms. Evans, I've been in business a long time. Do you want to know how I've made my success? By only investing in what I believe in. And I do not believe in the Hemlock Inn anymore."

"Wait, what are you saying? What does that mean?"

"I'm sorry, but I can't buy the Hemlock Inn. I'm pulling my offer."

The next few moments passed in a blur. He said a few

more things about why he'd made this decision, having run the numbers and decided it wasn't worth it anymore, but I barely heard any of it. There was a whooshing in my ears and my mind had gone blank. All I could see was Sylvia's disappointed face.

"I wish you luck with the inn," he said finally, standing and holding out his hand. I shook it on autopilot, barely noticing when he left the courtyard.

29

I walked back to the front desk, my mind blank. Someone had dropped off some invoices to be signed for various vendors, so I began working my way through the pile, my mind barely seeing what I was signing.

Tony Vasco didn't want to buy the inn. Guests were cancelling their reservations left and right. The bistro was the emptiest I'd seen it since I'd gotten to town. Tracy was still in jail. And I was stuck with an inn I didn't know how to run. What was I going to do now?

"Simone, I was just looking for you!" Camille approached, a smile lighting up her face. "So glad I found you. I'm finishing up some last-minute details for the event and I was hoping you could help choose something."

As she held out two different colored cloth napkins, asking me which one I preferred for the tables at the charity auction, I wondered where Camille had been. With the event only a few days away, and everything that was going on, I'd forgotten to look for her. She seemed determined to put on this event.

"This one," I said, picking the blue one. She smiled and

made a note in her small notepad, sticking the two napkins back in her giant purse.

"I'm glad you finally stopped by," I said. "Everything's been so crazy, I keep forgetting about the event. Where have you been?"

"Oh, taking care of a few different things," she said with a wave of her hand, her gaze down on her notepad. "There's always something to do when it comes to planning an event," she added with a laugh.

"Well, thanks for keeping me up to date," I said, thinking about the charity auction and all the ways I'd managed to fail Aunt Sylvia. I couldn't hide the sadness in my voice.

"Sweetie, what's wrong?" she asked, leaning forward and putting her hand over mine.

I sighed, unsure of how much to tell her, then opened my mouth and found everything pouring out of me. "I'm ruining this inn. I couldn't save the one seller Sylvia had, and Tracy's in jail, and now Angeline's dead... I wish I hadn't come here in the first place. You all would be so much better off without me."

"Oh, Simone, now that's not true! Yes, you've had some obstacles here, but that's what owning a business is all about. I'm just glad we'll still be able to put on the charity auction. I know that's what Bethany would want."

"You two were close, huh?"

"Pretty close," she said with a nod. "She could be... difficult, but who isn't these days?" Camille chuckled, her eyes softening as she focused on a memory. "Sometimes I wonder if things could've been different, you know? I mean, we knew each other for so long, and to have her taken like this... it puts things in perspective."

"What can you tell me about Victor?" I asked, not realizing this question was on my mind until the words were coming out of my mouth.

"What do you mean?" Camille asked.

"I mean, you were so close to Bethany. Were you close to Victor as well?"

Camille smiled, though it didn't quite reach her eyes. "We weren't as close, no. But I find sometimes, it's hard to be close to the person who marries your friend, you know? Not because you don't like them, or anything like that, but sometimes it's easier not to be close."

I thought about what she said then. I understood not being close to your friend's partner, but I thought it was odd that she considered it *easier* not to be close to them. Seemed like an odd reason to not be friends with someone who was important to your friend.

Why was I even still interested in Victor, or Bethany? Tony Vasco didn't want to buy the inn and I didn't know how I was going to find another buyer. Yet here I was, picking out napkins and sleuthing.

I couldn't help but want to help. This inn had entered my life at a time when I thought I had nothing left, and, even though there had been some bumps in the road—which was the biggest understatement I could've made—I still wanted to see this place be successful, and I wanted to find Bethany's killer.

It wasn't only Bethany's killer; it was Angeline's killer, too, and I couldn't stand the thought of those murders going unsolved. Like I had with that girlfriend who'd been crying at the bar, I wanted to help.

"Listen, I'm going on and on about all of this when we've got an event to finish planning," Camille said, interrupting my thoughts. "We'll stay in touch until this thing is finished. Thanks for all of your help."

"No problem. I'm happy to know someone is still thinking about this event."

Camille finished putting her things into her bag and slung it over her shoulder. "Any plans for the evening?"

I glanced out the window. The sun was setting, but it wouldn't be dark for a little while. Nadia was due any minute to take over the front desk, and I wanted to get outside and do something. "I think I might go for a jog. Help clear my thoughts."

"Better you than me," she said with a laugh. "I've never really been a runner. Always seems like you end up in the exact same place you started."

She smiled and said goodbye, and I waited for Nadia to arrive for her shift. Once she showed up, I left her to the front desk and headed upstairs to change.

As I changed into my running clothes, I thought more about what Camille had said. I hadn't realized how close she and Bethany were. It was clear Camille didn't want too many people to know about their friendship, as it hadn't come up for me with anyone else in my conversations with them.

In fact, no one had mentioned Camille at all. I still didn't know who had murdered Bethany, but I wondered if Camille knew more than she was letting on or even realized. She was swamped with planning this event, but I hoped I'd have time to talk to her more and see what she thought about everything.

I warmed up in the lobby and began my way down the road. I was feeling aimless and needed to get out into the fresh air to clear my mind. Hopefully, this quick jog would clear my head and something would break through.

My screw-up with Tony Vasco was still weighing on me. I'd tried to find Bethany's killer after it was clear the murder investigation made him nervous about buying the inn, but all I'd managed to do was find another dead body and lose his offer. Tracy was still gone, and who knew when she'd be back.

Could I find another buyer and turn everything around on my own?

30

T he wind rushed through my hair as my feet smacked the pavement. The sun began its slow decline, and I was grateful I'd grabbed a jacket before leaving the inn as a chill set in. For now, I focused on the road ahead of me and what this all meant for my future.

I didn't have a job back in California or a place to live. Was I really prepared to move back into my childhood bedroom and bunk with my parents?

It didn't feel like I had a choice at this point. They'd accept me back, no hesitation, but my mother would spend forever wondering what Aunt Sylvia had been thinking to leave me her inn and how bad a decision it was. She meant well, but she never felt like I was all that capable of taking on the world.

Of course, events of the past year kept proving her right. I wasn't interested in hearing about my failures every day for the next six months while I hunted for a job. I didn't want to have to explain what had happened at Antonio's bar, and I didn't know if I'd even be able to keep them from finding out.

Why had I punched that customer? Is that when everything went downhill for me? Things were not looking good for me back in California.

From behind me, the sound of a truck's motor brought my thoughts back to the present. I glanced over my shoulder and moved to the side of the road, giving the truck some space. I hadn't realized that I'd drifted out into the middle of the road.

Given how empty this road was, it shouldn't have been a big deal to be out in the middle of it, but I'd dealt with big trucks before and didn't want to give the driver any reason to focus on me.

The truck sped up, but rather than moving around me, it came closer to me. What was the driver doing? I quickened my pace and stepped onto the dirt at the edge of the shoulder, but the truck wouldn't stop.

Suddenly, I felt the truck tap against the back of my legs, and I lost my footing. With a scream, I tumbled into the underbrush along the side of the road.

I landed on my back with an *oomph* a few feet from the road and stared up at the sky. My body ached from the contact with the truck and the tumble into the ditch.

The truck revved its engine from the road, and I sat up to see if someone was coming after me. Instead, I heard the truck peel off in the direction we'd been heading. Guess they weren't interested in seeing if I was dead.

I lay back in the grass, watching the clouds drifting past overhead. The sun had set, and a chill was in the air. I didn't feel it on my skin, though. All I could feel was the adrenaline as it left my body.

My fingers tightened in the grass around me as my eyes filled with tears, the reality of this experience coming over me. A few clouds passed by and crickets chirped in the surrounding underbrush. I wondered if they knew what had happened here just now. Did I know what had happened?

Images flashed through my head, of Chrissy and my parents, the Adlers, and, oddly enough, Tracy. Fear coursed through my veins—had someone tried to kill me?

Blood rushed to my head as I sat up, and I held in the urge to throw up. I needed to get out of here before whoever had tried to kill me came back to finish the job. Was this just to scare me? If so, it had worked.

I stood and paused for a moment, checking to make sure that all my body parts could still move. Blood oozed from a cut on the back of my leg. I'd be sore in the morning, with more bruises than I could count.

I pulled off my jacket, pressed it against my leg, and wrapped it around the cut to stop the bleeding. I was grateful that I'd grabbed the jacket before leaving the inn. The inn probably had a first aid kit, so I could clean it up there.

The impact of what had happened hit me. Someone had tried to kill me. Someone had seen me running down the road and hit me with their car. There was no way they hadn't known what they were doing. Who was after me?

I didn't think I'd pissed anyone off enough to drive them to a homicidal rage. My teeth chattered as the cold air whipped against my bare arms. Were they still out there somewhere? I needed to get out of here, and fast.

I trudged through the underbrush and climbed the steep ditch, trying to find my way back to the road. The only reason someone would have to kill me would be if they thought I was getting too close to the truth about what had happened to Bethany and Angeline.

I tried to remember what the truck looked like or if I'd

gotten a glimpse of the driver. It had all happened so fast. All I could remember was that the truck was big and dark.

Who could've known I'd be out here? I'd told Camille and Nadia where I was going, but the person responsible could've just as easily been driving down the road when they saw me. Or maybe they'd been in the bistro and had overheard my announcement. Anyone could've done it.

I found the road and began my trek back up to the inn. There were no cars waiting for me. The would-be killer must've left. My body groaned in pain as I walked, fear now replaced with anger. Why had someone tried to kill me? I wasn't anywhere near finding out the truth about what had happened to Bethany or Angeline. And yet, someone had decided that I needed to be eliminated. What gave them the right to decide who lives and who dies in this town?

This trip to Pine Brook was turning out so much worse than I'd expected. I might not be able to sell the inn to Tony Vasco or anyone else, but I could find the killer and make them pay for what they'd done to us all.

31

B ack at the inn, I cleaned up my leg in my room, wiping it down with a cloth and running water over it in the sink. Blood ran down the drain in a swirl, turning my stomach along with it. I'd found the first aid kit in Sylvia's office and went straight upstairs, not wanting to talk to anyone.

I wanted some peace and quiet, but my grumbling stomach reminded me I hadn't eaten in hours. I grumbled to myself as I headed downstairs to the lobby, hoping I wouldn't see anyone as I snuck back into the bistro.

"You look awful." Tracy's voice startled me.

I hadn't seen her when I'd first entered the inn, and I almost didn't believe what I was seeing now. She was standing behind the front desk, helping check someone in. Lola sat next to her, licking her shoe.

I walked over to the front desk, not feeling my legs as I moved, wondering if she was a ghost. My body still shook from the impact of getting run off the road, and I knew my arms were trembling. My eyes welled up with tears as I walked over to her.

She looked up when I got close and finished up with the guest. "Nadia, will you keep an eye on things? I need to talk to Simone." She led me back to Sylvia's office, Lola following us.

"I don't understand," I said, once we were situated. "Why are you here?"

"I work here, silly," she said, her normally mocking tone softened. Her gaze swept to the bandages on my knees. "I meant what I said. You look awful. What happened?"

I don't know what came over me, but something propelled me to wrap my arms around Tracy and pull her into a hug. She let out a little *oomph* as I did, surprised by the gesture, but let me hug her and even patted my back, albeit awkwardly. I pulled away and stared up at her face, not surprised by the tears welling up in my eyes.

"Why are you here?" I asked, my voice cracking over the words as I held in my tears. "Did the police let you go?"

"We'll get to all of that," she said, waving her hand flippantly, her face now concerned. "What happened to you?"

I walked her through everything that had happened since I showed up in town; deciding to find Bethany's killer and not knowing what the hell I was doing; looking for suspects and not having any luck; finding the blackmail log and bringing them to the police; her arrest; and getting run off the road by a truck.

Tracy studied me closer. "So you think the killer was out in the truck, trying to get rid of you? Are you going to tell the police what happened?"

"I probably should, but I need to know what happened with you! Why are you here? Did the police release you?"

She nodded. "This morning, actually. Tate ran out of his forty-eight hours and had to let me go because he didn't have any actual evidence. There were a ton of other names on that blackmail log, so my lawyer argued it could've been anyone. I had to go pick up my cat from a friend, then I came straight here."

"Why was Bethany blackmailing you?"

Tracy's face paled a bit at my question, but she took a couple of deep breaths. "Your aunt and I weren't just business partners. We were in a relationship."

My eyes widened as her words registered in my brain. In a relationship? How did I not know this?

"What about Uncle Tim?" I asked, referring to my uncle, who had passed away a few years ago. "Did he know?"

Tracy shook her head. "I don't even think Sylvia knew when he was alive. Heck, I only figured it out after the funeral, personally. Or at least, we didn't know how strong our feelings were."

I stared at her in confusion, and she hurried to explain.

"We started noticing feelings for each other after he passed away. We were already spending so much time together, with the inn, and with Tim gone, it opened something up for us. Sylvia never would've cheated on him when he was alive, and she felt weird about her feelings when they first started. She almost felt like she was still cheating on him, even though we weren't doing anything. We spent many nights talking in here, trying to work through our feelings. We put them aside so we could keep working together like everything was normal, but we couldn't ignore how we were feeling. One day, it was like we had never been apart. We couldn't hide our feelings anymore."

I tried to keep my face neutral as she spoke, but this was blowing my mind. I had no idea about what Aunt Sylvia had been doing while she was up here. Clearly there was more going on than anyone in my family knew.

"No one else in town knows," Tracy said, continuing her

explanation. "We didn't want to make it into a whole big scandal thing, and Sylvia didn't want anyone to think less of Tim for it. No one would have cared that we were lovers—this town is open-minded—but we were private and didn't want to let anyone into our little world. I think we both enjoyed having the secret, something that no one else knew about and was just ours."

I nodded, understanding that urge. Sometimes you didn't want to let other people into the private parts of your life.

"Then, after Sylvia passed away, Bethany found some letters between the two of us," Tracy went on, darting her eyes away from mine at the mention of the letters. "We'd write each other these letters and slip them back and forth when we were working. They said the nicest things." Her gaze went a little fuzzy as she remembered the letters, a genuine love washing over her features.

She sighed and looked back up at me. "I don't even think Bethany realized what she had until I begged for them back. By that point, she wanted to see how much money she could get out of me. I was gathering the first payment to give to her when she was killed."

I sat back, letting her words filter through my brain. That was a good motive for murder; I could understand why the police had arrested her. Still, they must've realized it wasn't a good enough motive to charge her. Sure, she didn't enjoy working with Bethany, and she probably felt worse about her after she started blackmailing her, but that didn't mean she killed Bethany.

Tracy leaned forward then, putting her hand over mine. "I'm sorry for not saying anything sooner about your aunt. It seemed weird to bring anyone into our little secret."

"Why did you hate me so much when I first showed up?"

I asked, building up the courage to ask the question that had been bugging me since I'd arrived in town.

To my surprise, Tracy's eyes filled with tears, and she looked away. "I'm sorry. I really am. It's just... you look so much like Sylvia. I was, and still am, so sad about her death. I hadn't been able to process my feelings because I wasn't supposed to love her. No one was supposed to know about us, so how could I grieve? I know that's an excuse, but I couldn't help it. Then, once you showed up, it was like a switch was flipped. I realized that I'd lost the love of my life, and someone new was coming in to tell me how to run things. I didn't know if you were going to sell the inn, but I figured you'd thought about it, and I put up a wall. I'm sorry for the way I treated you."

I nodded, her words making sense. I could understand why she'd respond to my presence the way she had. I wished she'd said something sooner, but I understood where she was coming from.

It was easy to forgive her in that moment, knowing all that she had been through since Sylvia had passed away, all those feelings and emotions she couldn't express. It can cut you up inside to hold in that amount of pain.

"Did you tell the police all this?" I asked, still wondering how she'd gotten out of jail.

"I did," she said, nodding. "When I told my lawyer all of this, he advised me to be honest with the police. I didn't want to say anything at first, because Tate has never liked me. We went to high school together, and I turned him down for a date. Plus, a few years ago, he got drunk and called me, begging me to date him. I was less nice in my rejection that time. This was before he became chief of police, of course." She rolled her eyes, and I had to agree— as if that excused his actions. What a creep!

"I don't think he's gotten over those incidents," Tracy went on. "I didn't want to open up to him about what had happened. But after talking with my lawyer and speaking with Detective Patel, I figured I should say something."

"What did you tell the police? That Bethany had been blackmailing you? I'd imagine that would make them more likely to think you had done it."

"I told them that, but also, I'm pretty sure I'm not the only person Bethany was blackmailing. From the way the police responded to that information, I get the sense they have evidence someone else was involved as well. Plus, they found a witness at the inn who remembers seeing me that night. He'd come down for a late-night snack, and we'd chatted for a while. He'd left town and the number we had for him was wrong, so it took the police a little while to find him."

What if they hadn't found that witness? I shuddered just thinking about it. Tracy might still have been in jail.

"Tony Vasco pulled his offer," I blurted out. "I tried to convince him not to, but he wouldn't listen. But now that you're not in jail, maybe he'd be more open to buying the inn?"

Tracy smiled. "Don't worry. The Hemlock has made it all these years. It'll survive without a buyer."

I returned her smile, but my heart wasn't in it. I didn't want to see this place just survive; I wanted to see it thrive.

32

Thirty minutes later, I was sitting across from Detective Patel in one of the interview rooms at the police station. She'd hurried me into the back when I'd shown up, as if she hadn't wanted anyone to know I was here. I didn't mind; I didn't want Chief Tate to know I was here, either.

After Tracy had opened up to me, I'd sent Patel a text, asking if we could meet so I could report a crime. Though I hadn't been badly injured, I'd still been attacked by a car, and it was too much of a coincidence for it to not be related to Bethany and Angeline's deaths. Their killer was trying to get rid of me, or at least scare me, and I was going to do what I could to catch them. It was late, but I needed to talk to Patel.

"All right, tell me what happened," Patel said, flipping open her notepad to a clean page.

"I went for a run this afternoon. Down the main road away from the inn. A truck approached me from behind and followed me for a few minutes. I tried to move out of its way, but it kept coming after me. Finally, it clipped my back legs.

I tripped and fell into the weeds on the side of the road. I think the driver would've come after me, but another car showed up, so they drove away."

"Are you okay?" She scanned my body, as if looking for injuries.

"A little scraped up, but I'll be fine."

"Did you see the driver?"

I shook my head. "It all happened so fast."

"What about the make or model of the car?"

"It was dark and big. Definitely a truck."

"Do you know how many people own trucks in the area?" She hadn't written anything down.

I leaned forward, losing my patience. "Someone came after me with their truck. If that other car hadn't driven up, I'd probably be dead right now. You've already got two dead women on your hands; are you really willing to have another?"

She sighed. "Look, I understand this was probably very scary. I'll take down your statement and file a police report, but I don't see how this has anything to do with those other murders. You might've simply been in the wrong place at the wrong time."

This was getting me nowhere. I agreed to file the report, hoping that if we at least had something on the record, the police would believe me more if some other attack happened. Patel took down all my information, then led me out of the room and back to the front of the police station.

We entered the front waiting area of the station, where a woman was sitting behind the front desk, typing at the computer. She glanced up as we entered.

"Have you talked to Damian?" I asked. "He came to see me, and he said he was going to come to the police."

Patel turned to me. "Yes, I spoke with him. His alibi

checks out. He was nowhere near Pine Brook when Bethany was killed."

"What about Victor? I talked to him after Tracy was arrested, and he got very angry with me. I think he might've gotten angry enough to hurt his wife, too."

"I heard about your altercation. You're lucky he isn't pressing charges against you for harassment. Look, I can't say anything else about an active case. We're pursuing multiple lines of inquiry, and you'd be smart to keep your nose out of things." She left then, heading back into the police station.

This visit had been a waste of time. That police report wasn't likely to find the truck driver, and I hadn't learned anything useful about the murder investigation. I was no closer to finding the real killer than when I'd shown up.

"You're Simone, aren't you?" The woman at the front desk had stood from her seat. "I'm friends with Estelle," she said when I looked over at her. "I'm Miriam."

Ah, yes. Estelle had mentioned she knew someone at the police station, her hair stylist's mother. I walked over to the front desk. Miriam looked to be in her sixties, with greying hair in a low bun and lines around her eyes that deepened when she smiled.

"Patel is like that with everyone," Miriam went on. "She gets really protective over her cases."

"I wish she would tell me something. I'm not trying to get in the way of her investigation, but I want to find the killer, too."

Miriam glanced over her shoulder, but we were alone. "I probably shouldn't say this," she whispered, leaning across the desk. "But they've got a warrant to search Victor's home. I don't think he's off their suspect list."

"Really?" What had they found that led to a warrant? "Do you know anything else?"

Miriam shook her head. "I hope they find the killer soon."

"Thanks for that information," I said. I left the station, thinking about what evidence they had to justify a warrant for Victor's home. Would they find something inside that pointed to him as the killer?

33

The next morning, I was up early. I was pleased to see the sun shining, but I knew I wasn't running today. Not only was I still sore from the day before, but I was scared. I didn't know if that truck was still out there, or if the person driving it still wanted to get rid of me. I didn't want to take my chances.

I changed into jeans and a white t-shirt and sat at Sylvia's vanity table for a moment, staring into the mirror. I touched a small cut on my jaw from yesterday's incident, wincing slightly at the pain. Would it leave a scar?

I glanced down at the vanity, at a small bottle of perfume pushed back into the corner, near the mirror. I pulled it out and spritzed it into the air, inhaling Sylvia's scent. I was transported back in time, to the last time I'd had a cut at the Hemlock Inn, and Sylvia had patched up my knee.

"There, now, all better," she'd said, pressing a bandage against my knee and sitting back on her heels. She was crouched in front of me, tending to my wound. I was six, my hair in pigtails, my cheeks tear-stained.

I remembered sniffling. "Why does it hurt so much?" I had asked her, my small voice catching on the words.

Sylvia had smiled and held her hand against my cheek, the cheek which now hurt from the cut. "Sometimes life hurts. It happens to all of us. But what matters is that we always get back up and try again. Can you try again for me, my dear?"

I remembered nodding and pulling her neck into a hug, pressing my face against the crook of her neck and breathing in the scent that was now wafting through the room. My eyes welled up with tears at the memory. Just like she told me back then, I needed to get back up and try again.

I drifted down the stairs to the lobby, heading back to the bistro. Everything was humming along nicely. The guests seemed happy, food was coming in and out of the kitchen at a steady pace, and there didn't seem to be any issues from anyone. Lola trotted along beside some new guests, who gave her a pat on the head as they walked past me. I smiled as I saw them go.

I began walking around the tables, nodding to guests as I passed, surprised by how many people I recognized. When I'd first shown up at the inn, just a week ago—had it really only been that long?—I hadn't known a single person.

Now, people were smiling as I approached, and I had a short conversation with a couple of them as I passed tables. I was going to miss this, being recognized when I walked into a room and having brief conversations with people I was beginning to know.

I had nothing like this back in California, and while a week ago I wouldn't have thought I wanted something like this, now I was enjoying it more than I expected. It helped me feel welcome and safe and appreciated in the space that

I was in, and I'd been missing out on that back in California the past couple of years.

Losing my job and my apartment had taken a toll on me, and even though there was a killer out there wanting to see me dead, Pine Brook had woven some kind of spell over me. I didn't want to leave, even after the events of the last night. Plus, I was really starting to feel like I could handle some of the responsibilities of the inn. I'd kept things running while Tracy was gone, and people seemed happy to be here.

I made my way into the kitchen, which was bustling and smelled delicious. Javier roamed around, carrying back empty plates and filling fresh orders. He gave me a wink as he passed me. I drifted over to the stove, passing the new sink which had been installed that morning. At the stove, Hank was stirring something in a big pot. He smiled as I walked up to him.

"Taste this," he said, scooping out a bit of the stuff from the pot and holding out the spoon. I eyed the orange mixture, hesitating, then ate the whole thing.

"Wow! This is amazing," I said, wiping the corners of my mouth. "What is it?"

"Peach drizzle," Hank said, stirring the pot again. "I'm thinking about pouring it over the berry cobbler. Nice contrast and mix of flavors for dessert. Do you think people will like it?"

"I think people will love it." I grinned, hoping I'd get an order of dessert before it sold out. The kitchen seemed to hum under Hank's guidance. There weren't any more falls or spills, and it felt like he was directing a symphony while mixing the pot.

"You've really got a handle on everything here, huh?" I asked. To my surprise, the tips of his ears and his cheeks turned pink.

"I don't know about that," he said, looking down into the pot. Then he looked up at me and a smile broke across his face. "Do you really think so?"

I smiled and leaned forward. "Absolutely. People have been raving about your food all day. I don't know why you weren't brought in sooner. Pierre was great and all, but he made too much French food. I don't think Pine Brook was ready for it."

Hank shrugged, still smiling and blushing. "He wasn't so bad. He taught me a lot. Well, not exactly taught. He didn't let me get too close to the stove when he was cooking since I accidentally burned his hand that one time. But I spent a lot of time watching, and I saw the way he made cooking into an art form. I've been trying to replicate that. It's magical."

"It really is," I said, admiring the bustling kitchen.

Just then, Estelle popped her head into the kitchen door and squealed when she saw me. She hurried over, waving her hands in front of her.

"Simone, Simone!" she said, practically crashing into me in her excitement. "Is it true? Oh, tell me it's true, it must be true?"

"What?" I asked, laughing as she tried not to slip in her kitten heels. "What's true?"

"Tracy's back?" she asked, her voice hopeful. "Did you find Bethany's killer?"

I pressed my index finger to my lips to shush her. I still didn't want it getting out that I'd been asking around about Bethany's killer, even though half the town probably knew because I'd accused the other half of the town of murder. Hank was back to stirring his drizzle, though I thought I saw tilt his head in our direction, as if he were waiting to hear my response.

"Why don't we leave Hank alone and go sit outside?" I suggested, steering Estelle away from the stove.

I wanted to tell her everything that had been going on since she and her husband were the reason I'd gotten into this mess in the first place, but I didn't want it to get around town yet. I knew eventually people would find out, because nothing was a secret here, but this way at least slowed down the pace a bit.

I led Estelle through the bistro and into the courtyard. She was practically shaking with excitement to hear what I had to say. Lola came to follow us, giving Estelle's hand a lick as we got settled in.

"Where's Miles?" I asked, looking around for her husband.

Estelle waved her hand flippantly. "He got caught up in a game of chess at the park, and I didn't want to wait around for him before getting the news. Now tell me what's going on!"

"Yes, Tracy is back," I said, once we were situated in a private area. "The police still don't know who killed Bethany, but they at least don't suspect Tracy anymore." I paused then, wondering how much else to say, then decided to go for it.

I explained about the blackmail log—not getting specific about Tracy's relationship with Sylvia, as that wasn't my secret to tell, but that Bethany was blackmailing people—and my run-in with that truck. Estelle listened, her face moving from surprise to shock to horror.

"Are you all right?" she asked, examining me for any injuries. I was glad I'd worn jeans to cover up the scrapes.

"I'm okay," I said, touched by her concern but not wanting the focus on me. "I wish I knew who was doing all this. It's like I can see the puzzle in front of me, and it's missing one piece. If I could find that one piece, I know I'd have the answer."

Estelle was quiet for a moment. "It sounds like you should let the police handle things from here on out. Now that Tracy's back, couldn't you leave? Wouldn't it be safer if you left since someone tried to kill you?"

She had a good point, I couldn't deny that. With Tracy back, the inn could go on. But Sylvia had left me the inn for a reason, hadn't she? Maybe she wanted more for me here than just to sell it.

"I don't know how to explain it," I said finally. "I get what you're saying, and I've thought about it myself too. It's gotten dangerous here in Pine Brook. But I don't know. Something about this town, about this inn, has drawn me in. I don't feel ready to leave yet."

"I know exactly what you mean," Estelle said, patting my hand. "Miles and I came here years ago. I was in love with a man and willing to follow him wherever he wanted to go. Now that our kids are grown and out of the house, we've thought about going back to our family on the East Coast. But there's something about this place that takes hold of your heart and doesn't let go."

I smiled at her words, realizing she'd described it exactly the way I couldn't. I wanted to see things through here. There was more going on with murders, and I wanted to help however I could. Plus, knowing how close Tracy and my aunt had been, I wanted to know more about Sylvia and what she was like in her later years. I hoped Tracy would tell me one day.

34

Two days later, the big event was here. I'd spent the last two days helping with the final preparations and thinking about Bethany's murder. I woke up early that morning, butterflies in my stomach. I was excited to see the charity auction come to life, but I also knew the killer might still be out there somewhere. I hoped Patel would find them soon.

The inn was a flurry of activity when I came downstairs. It was slowly coming to life, and I forgot about the murder investigation for a moment as I imagined what the place would look like in a few hours' time.

We'd put so much work into this event, it needed to go well. Even if the inn wasn't mine after it ended, I wanted to see this event successful. It seemed the least we could do for Sylvia, and for Bethany, and for Angeline.

Tracy directed the moving pieces all around her at the front desk. Tables were set up, chairs unstacked, place settings and placards put where they needed to go.

We were at a limited capacity for guests at the inn to accommodate the event, so at least there wasn't any checking in that needed to happen this morning. I hurried over to the front desk, eager to talk to Tracy and see how I could help.

"Morning, sunshine," she said once I came into view. She'd swept her hair up off her neck and her eyes were bright. I had a feeling she was much happier to be here than at the police station in jail. I was so happy she was back.

"What can I do to help?" I asked, as she continued to direct all the things around her. She was quite a sight to behold. I didn't want to interrupt her flow, but I wanted to be useful.

"Everything is running pretty smoothly out here," she said, not taking her eyes off the symphony of event planning happening in front of her. "Maybe go check with Hank, see if he needs any help." She flicked her eyes over at me. "I still can't believe you hired him to take over the kitchen."

Rather than shrink away, I held my ground and met her gaze. "It was the right thing to do at the time. Pierre had left, and Hank was the only one who volunteered." I'd spent too much time concerned about whether I could run this place; I wasn't going to let Tracy make me question my decisions.

To my surprise, she broke out in a smile. "It was the right thing to do. I wish I'd thought of it sooner. His turnovers are delicious. I've already had three this morning," she added with a wink.

I returned her smile. It was starting to feel like she was happy I was here at the inn. We'd had such a great chat about my aunt and their close relationship; I hoped we could keep that going.

I hurried off to the kitchen to see if Hank had something for me to help with. Maybe I could sneak one of his turnovers, too.

Fortunately, there was just as much going on inside the

kitchen as outside, and Hank gave me some duties to prepare for this evening. Penny and Eddy kept the tables moving along, while Javier spent his time getting the food ready for the event that night. We'd hired some extra catering staff to help with the event, and they showed up in the afternoon.

The rest of the day passed by in a blur as we all hustled to get everything ready. As time flew by, I couldn't stop thinking about Bethany.

The only reason we were here was because this event was her baby, her pride and joy. She'd done all the work to make it possible for us to put on something so amazing. And she wasn't here to appreciate it. It broke my heart. I was even more determined to figure out who had killed her, and who had killed Angeline.

Did I think Victor was the murderer? There was always a chance. Spouses were most likely to kill their spouse out of all other people. But he'd seemed so distraught when I'd first gone to see him. Were those tears of an innocent man or a man upset with himself for having killed his wife?

He had gotten angry with me when I'd started questioning whether Tracy had killed Bethany. I'd seen some genuine aggression in his eyes.

That still didn't explain why Angeline was killed. Did I really believe that she was a victim of a robbery? Or did she know something she wasn't supposed to, and someone had to get rid of her?

Mid-day, I was in Sylvia's office, staring at the financial spreadsheets Ron had given me a few days ago. I'd finally decided it was time I reviewed the inn's situation and try to come up with something to do about it. Tony Vasco wasn't interested in the Hemlock Inn anymore, but there had to be other buyers out there.

Part of me wondered if maybe *I* was the right person to take over the Hemlock, but I pushed that thought away. I wasn't cut out for running an inn.

I hoped the spreadsheets—which were already giving me a headache, like the time I studied abroad in Spain and stared at a dinner menu for twenty minutes as the words swam in front of me, unintelligible and mocking my rudimentary knowledge of the language—would shed some light on the financial future of the inn.

Three glass jars of stones sat on the windowsill next to me and reflected the light from the sun into the room. I'd found more jars as I went through Sylvia's office and had taken to placing them around me.

A knock at the door pulled me away from the spreadsheets, and I was grateful for the interruption. Ron popped his head around the door and I waved him in.

"I was just going over the paperwork you shared," I said, motioning to the stack in front of me. "I'm trying to make heads or tails out of all of it."

"Yes, it is rather complicated," Ron said, holding an envelope in front of him. He didn't take a seat, and he wouldn't look me in the eye.

"Is everything okay?" I asked, sitting up in my chair. The spreadsheets had caused me to slide down in the seat until I was almost horizontal with the desk.

Ron glanced down at the envelope in his hands, then back up at me. "I promise this was purely an accident. My filing system leaves something to be desired. Theresa keeps telling me I need to go digital and put everything on my computer, but I miss the feel of actual paper. We don't appreciate the original copies, you know?"

I had thought it was strange that Ron had given me paper copies of the inn's financials, rather than a digital version. I'd assumed my aunt had preferred paper copies, but I never imagined that Ron could make it as a lawyer with hard copies.

He took a step forward and placed the envelope on the desk. I saw my name written across the front and looked up at him for an explanation.

"Your aunt left this for you. It must've gotten mixed up with the rest of the paperwork for her estate. I only just now found it, when I was going through her files to close it out. She wanted me to give it to you when you first showed up in town. I'm sorry for not bringing it to you sooner. Can you ever forgive me? I'm going straight back to my office after this, so Theresa and I can start digitizing everything." He shuddered at the word "digitizing." "I won't let this happen again."

"It's okay," I said, picking up the envelope and staring at my name. I recognized Sylvia's handwriting from all the birthday cards she'd written me over the years. "We all make mistakes."

Ron visibly sagged at my words, the tension leaving his body in a wave. "Thank goodness. I'll leave you alone with that. See you tonight."

He left the room and quietly shut the door behind him, but I barely heard him go as I stared at the letter.

Sylvia had written me a letter before she died. And she'd asked Ron to hold on to it until I came to Washington. Would this reveal the answers to every question I'd had about her since I showed up in town?

Not giving myself time to process what I was about to discover, I ripped open the envelope and read the pages that tumbled out.

Dear Simone,

I hope you can forgive me for how everything has played out.

Do you remember those movies we would watch when you were a kid, when you and Chrissy would visit and want to stay up late? The movies where a detective gathers all the suspects in one room and perfectly explains how everything happened? I suppose I likened myself to one of those detectives, and this is me gathering you in a room and revealing all.

If you're reading this, it means I'm dead, and the Hemlock Inn is yours. What a twist, right? It's been, what, eighteen years since you've even thought of Pine Brook? And now I'm giving you an inn to run? Talk about a surprise ending.

All right, enough of the movie references. It's time I get serious. As serious as one can be when one is diagnosed with terminal cancer and only has a few short weeks to live.

Tell your mother I'm sorry for not reaching out sooner, and that I'm sorry for all the years we went without speaking. The truth of why this happened is buried deep, but I hope she can learn to unearth her skeletons and make peace with our history. I know I have. You'll have to ask her about it one day.

I always thought you had true greatness inside of you, even if you couldn't see it yourself. I knew Chrissy would stick to her plan, marry a great man, build a family, and create a great career for herself. She's a professor, isn't that right? I always knew she'd figure it out. Just like your mother figured out her true destiny, too. We have some pretty strong women in our family.

As for you, well... I always thought you were more like me. A little lost, a little unsure. Chrissy walked through the world with confidence seeped into her bones, while you kept your eyes open and saw what others didn't want to see. Never one to back down from a fight, am I right?

My thoughts flew back to that scene at the bar, punching a customer because he'd been hurting his girlfriend. Sounds like Aunt Sylvia had seen that fire in me, even as a kid. I kept reading.

Well, here's the greatest fight you'll ever face. If I'm right, you're lost right now and looking for some direction. This inn, this place where I found my greatest love, more than once, can give you that direction, if you'll let it.

This town is full of some truly great souls, and the Hemlock Inn attracts some of the most interesting people I've ever met. I believe you can find true happiness here, because it's where I found my happiness.

I know there's a buyer interested in this old place. He's a nice man, though he's got some odd ideas about what travelers want. He'd do fine with this inn. But, if I'm being honest, I hope you'll think about staying. This business could be good for you.

You might be wondering why your sister's name isn't in my will. I hope she wasn't too upset about that. I know she has a family and responsibilities, and I knew you'd be more open to coming back to the inn.

I figure, if you do decide to sell the inn, you can split the proceeds with your sister. Maybe put some money aside for your niece. Or, you can do what I hope you'll decide to do: stay in Pine Brook and run the Hemlock Inn.

Be kind to your parents and your sister, and give Lola a kiss for me. And remember: we're all so much stronger than we think. Have confidence that what you have chosen in this life is the right path for you.

Love, to the moon and back,

Aunt Sylvia

Tears streamed down my cheeks as I finished the letter. I stared down at the desk, tracing the lines in the wood that Sylvia had stared at every day of her life. And now she was gone, and she'd left me this last message, this last sign that I was in the right place.

Sylvia wanted me to run the inn. She didn't exclude Chrissy from her will because she was malicious or forgetful, but because she wanted to give me a chance for a new life. I was a big a fan of second chances.

What did Sylvia mean about why she and my mom hadn't spoken in years? As far as I knew, they had just grown apart as adults. But now that I thought about it, all the times my mom had talked about Aunt Sylvia when I was a kid, I couldn't actually remember her saying anything specific about what had happened between them.

My mom had made it seem like time and distance were at fault, but according to Sylvia, there were secrets buried here. Was there more going on than I realized?

Two people walked past Sylvia's door, chatting, and I was brought back to the present. There was a secret here that I wanted to unearth, but now wasn't the time. I stood, folding the letter back into the envelope and sticking it in the desk drawer. Right now, I had an inn to run.

35

Finally, the charity auction began like clockwork. So many people showed up, more than normal since word of Bethany's death was all anyone could talk about these days. Fortunately, all these people meant more bidders on the items, which would benefit the organization so much.

I spotted Lola standing with a few kids, getting pets and wearing a green bowtie. I was surprised that she was here, but Tracy had said that she was usually calm during these kinds of things and liked to be around the action.

Tracy beamed as she greeted guests, so pleased at the turnout. I was happy I could partake in the charity auction. Everyone looked amazing, and the decorations were wonderful.

Hank's appetizers were making the rounds on platters, and I eyed a few from a distance as I sipped my champagne. Artwork from local artists was set up around the main area of the inn, and people walked around, looking at each item and putting down bids.

Ron chatted with Camille, and I recognized a couple

other people that he had pointed out as being on the Board of Directors with Camille and Bethany. Where were they when we'd been planning this whole event? Seemed like they enjoyed showing up once everything was taken care of.

Nick was grabbing some food from the buffet, and I went over to say hello. He looked dashing in a tuxedo with a bowtie, though I noticed a couple white smudges on his lapel.

"Got something there," I said by way of greeting, reaching out and wiping at his lapel.

He laughed and glanced down, smoothing out the tux. His cheeks were pink. "I've been baking, and I couldn't help myself before I left. I had to give the bread one more roll before I could come here. I'm trying out a new sourdough starter and I'm worried I did something wrong."

"You bake, too?" I raised my eyebrows. "Is there anything you can't do?"

"Tie a bowtie," he said, leaning forward and folding his bowtie to the side, exposing the clip in the back. "I watched a ton of videos about how to do it, but gave up after ten tries and finally bought one of these."

"We all have our weaknesses," I said with a wink and a smile. His laugh sent something warm up my spine.

"You look great too," he said, gesturing to my dress.

I smiled and smoothed down the light purple fabric. Estelle had taken me shopping the day before once it became clear that none of the dresses I'd brought were appropriate for the charity auction.

I'd chosen a knee-length satin number, with a scoop neck and low back. I wore my thick curls loose, spending an hour that day scrunching them into shape and praying that nothing would cause them to poof out.

"Thank you," I said to Nick, smiling. "I always forget how much I enjoy dressing up until there's an excuse to do so."

"I heard about your run-in with that car," he said after a moment, his face turning serious. "Are you all right?"

I nodded, not the least bit shocked that this had gotten around town. It was harder than I thought to keep secrets in Pine Brook.

"Just a couple scratches, but nothing I can't handle. I'm pleased you could make it tonight."

"I wouldn't miss it for the world," Nick said. "The art center is a great organization, and I know Sylvia put a lot of work into making this possible. Even if she couldn't be here to see it all come together."

Just then, Hank called out for Nick across the room. We said goodbye, promising to catch up later, and I watched him walk away. He really did fit into that tux very nicely.

"This event is pretty impressive."

I looked up and saw Tony Vasco standing nearby, surveying the crowd. He smiled when he caught my eye, and we clinked our drinks together in a cheers.

"I'm amazed we got it all done in time." I took a sip of my drink. "I don't know if my aunt realized how much work it would take to put on a charity auction."

"I didn't know her well, but she seemed like the kind of person who'd love a big event like this. I bet she's watching you now, so proud."

My cheeks warmed at his compliment, Sylvia's letter burning a hole in my pocket. I'd kept it on me all night.

"I didn't expect to see you here," I said to Tony. "I figured you'd have left town by now."

"I heard there'd be some good items at the charity auction. Plus, I love supporting kids." He looked out over the crowd, his gaze thoughtful. "I must say, this is all very impressive. The Hemlock Inn may be able to survive this murder investigation after all. I understand the police are getting close to making an arrest?"

I kept silent, simply shrugging. I wasn't going to go around blathering about the police's progress.

"Yes, it's very impressive, all around," he went on. "I gotta say, I'm starting to regret pulling my offer. Any chance you'd still be interested?"

My eyes nearly bugged out of my face. "Are you serious?"

Tony shrugged, like it was no big deal to him either way. "I know a good opportunity when I see one, and I'm not afraid to put myself out there. You managed to turn everything around; I'd like to take the inn off your hands."

I turned back to the crowd, turning his words over in my head. Just a few short days ago, I would've jumped at the opportunity to have his offer back. But now? Now, things had changed. I'd changed.

Did I want to see the Hemlock Inn lose its personality and turn into a cookie-cutter B&B like all the others? Or was I willing to stand up and fight for its future?

"I'm not so sure about your offer anymore," I said slowly. "I haven't decided what I want to do with this place. Why don't we talk about it after the event?"

He raised a questioning eyebrow at me, then nodded. "Of course. You know where to find me. I think I see some delicious canapés over there." With that, he veered off to one of the side tables and left me alone.

"I'm always surprised to see how well everyone cleans up around here." Estelle slipped in beside me, with Miles in tow.

"You're not looking so bad yourself," I said, eyeing her green dress and his charcoal suit.

Estelle smirked. "Thanks. Gotta keep the boys looking." She winked at her husband, whose cheeks turned pink.

"This event is the best one we've ever put on, and we know you played a big role in all of this," Estelle went on, pulling me into a hug. "We're so pleased you're here."

My eyes teared up at her words. I was really starting to feel like this was the right place for me.

"What's going on over there?" Miles asked, pointing to the other side of the room.

Estelle and I looked over to the front door, where a small crowd had gathered. We drifted over, interested in what was going on.

To my surprise, Damian walked into the lobby, looking very dashing in a suit, his hair washed and slicked back from his head. He looked around, his eyes unsure, as if he was questioning whether it was a good idea to have shown up.

I wondered how many people in this room knew about his relationship with Bethany, and the fights they'd had before her death. While he wasn't a suspect in the police's eyes, did that automatically mean the town of Pine Brook would welcome him with open arms? Or would they reject him because he was from out of town and different?

"Damian," someone called. "So lovely to finally meet you." To my surprise, Tracy worked her way through the crowd over to Damian, grasping him by the arms and smiling. He visibly relaxed under her gaze, and other townspeople walked up, smiling and shaking his hand.

Seemed like he was getting that acceptance he'd finally been looking for. It was too bad that his half-sibling had been murdered, but he was getting what he'd hoped to find in town.

"I heard the police brought Victor back in for more

questioning," Estelle said, turning away from the gathering in front of us. "Think he did it?"

"Where did you hear that?" I asked. Miriam had said they were getting a warrant for his house. What had the police found when they searched it?

"We have our ways," Estelle said with a smile.

"I don't know," I said with a shrug, answering her initial question. "He seems suspicious, but I still feel like there's a missing piece. It doesn't make sense, but I don't know what the right answer is. I wish I could see it in front of me, you know?"

"I do," Miles said with a nod, studying the crowd. "Do you think it's someone out there?"

I watched the crowd with them. Was Bethany's killer out there? Was the person who'd run me off the road out there? Signs pointed to yes, if that person wasn't Victor, but I didn't know where to start.

Things had finally gotten good with Tracy back, but it felt like we were back at square one with Bethany's murder. How could we be sure Victor really was the killer?

36

I stood over the crowd, watching the festivities. Miles and Estelle had gone off to refill their drinks. Pine Brook was growing on me, and I was happy I could be here for the charity auction.

I didn't know what was going to happen with the inn, or what the next few days would bring, but I was glad I could be here and that Tracy wasn't in jail anymore. She'd already opened up to me so much, and I looked forward to talking with her more.

"Simone! There you are!" Camille called as she stepped out of the kitchen. "Mind helping me with something?" She was holding a covered tray and looking glamorous in a full-length, gold sequined dress.

"Hank made macaroons and wants to get them set up in the secondary room, but all the servers are busy now," she explained, gesturing to the tray she was holding. "I figured I'd set them up myself, but when I saw how many there were, I thought it might make sense to get some help. As long as you're not busy," she added, seeming to note that I'd been standing and staring at the crowd.

I smiled. "Of course not, I'm happy to help." I stepped forward and took the tray from her. "Lead the way." I'd been doing a lot of nothing for most of the night, and it felt good to finally help.

As we walked across the main room to the secondary room, we passed by Tracy, and I let her know where we were headed. She nodded and turned back to Damian, who was entertaining a group with a story about Bethany. He glanced over at us, his eyes landing on Camille for a moment, but then he turned back to the crowd.

We entered the secondary room, and Camille shut the door to give us some quiet. We started setting out the desserts onto the tables set up in this room, which guests would come into at the end of the event. Hank had made some delicious macaroons that everyone was going to love.

"Hank has done an excellent job," Camille said, studying the desserts and nodding her head approvingly. "When someone said Pierre had quit, and you'd replaced him with the busboy, I was certain it was going to be a disaster."

"So was I," I said with a chuckle. "But he's surprised us all. This entire event has been spectacular. You're going to raise so much money and it's amazing."

Camille smiled. "I appreciate that. I still can't believe we managed to put the whole thing on. While Bethany and I were co-chairs, she really ran with this event each year and did the bulk of the planning. I didn't know how things were going to turn out without her here, but it seems like it's been a success."

"How are you handling her death? I imagine she was a big part of your life, given how much you worked together and how long you'd known each other," I said, remembering what she had told me a few days before.

Camille nodded, her gaze focused on the treats in front of her as she organized them on a platter. "I'm doing okay with everything. It's been tough, but I know it's been so much tougher for Victor. I keep meaning to go over to his place and see how he's doing, but it feels like intruding, you know?"

My forehead crinkled. "I thought you said you've known Victor for a while as well? I don't think you'd be intruding."

Camille stopped setting out the treats, as if my words were taking a moment to register in her head. Then she smiled and continued placing the desserts. "Well, I was always closer to Bethany. I'm sure you know what that's like when someone close to you is in a relationship. You're close to the other person, but it's not quite the same. And I can't even imagine losing your spouse like this. I should go over and check on him."

"What was Bethany like when you were younger?" I asked, arranging the macaroons on the platter.

Camille's smile softened. "Similar to how she was as an adult. Always running around with a new scheme up her sleeve. She always wanted things to go exactly her way, and she wasn't interested in hearing alternatives. But she could be kind, too. She was a good friend to me when my parents divorced. It's hard to give up that kind of relationship when you get older, you know? The other person knows you so well, it's like you can't stop talking to them." She took a step closer to me, to set out the remaining desserts on my side of the tray.

"It's nice to have such a close friend as an adult," I said. "I'm sorry you had to lose her this way." I moved back to Camille's side, straightening the macaroons on the table as she continued setting them down.

A scent caught my nose, and I leaned in close to the treats, trying to follow the smell. Had Hank used some kind of floral mixture in the macaroons?

No, they just smelled like almonds and icing. I leaned away and sniffed the air. Where was that coming from? And what did it remind me of?

"Thanks. It's tough, but I'm getting through it," Camille said, interrupting my sniffing. She turned her attention back to the desserts.

My blood turned cold in my veins. It suddenly occurred to me where I'd smelled that floral scent. In Angeline's house, before stumbling onto her dead body. Had Camille been there? Were the two of them meeting for charity auction business? Or something more sinister?

I slowly looked up at Camille, trying to keep my expression steady. She was continuing to put out the treats, her attention down in front. Suddenly, she looked up at me and smiled when she saw me looking. I sent a forced smile back.

I couldn't accuse Camille of anything. I didn't know anything—all I had was the memory of a scent. I glanced back at the door, where music pumped in from the next room. She wouldn't hurt me while the entire town was so close, would she? Could I get her to tell me the truth, then call for help?

"Well, it looks like we did it," I said, stepping back from the table. "We've somehow pulled this off without Bethany and Angeline." I wiped my hands on a napkin. "Speaking of Angeline...have you heard any updates on what happened to her? I guess the gossip pipeline skipped over me."

"Not really. I haven't asked about it. She was a sweet girl. I'm sorry to hear what's happened to her."

"It sounds like the police thought it might be a robbery."

My voice filled the empty room, reminding me of how alone we were. "Had you talked to her recently?"

"Not for a few days, I don't think. I hope they find whoever killed her. If it was a robbery, they're probably long gone by now."

Camille took a step closer to me, and her perfume overwhelmed me. My stomach tightened as the truth came over me. According to the police, Angeline hadn't been dead for very long when I found her, which meant the scent hanging in the air hadn't had time to dissipate.

I strained to keep from throwing up, the image of Angeline's dead eyes seared in my memory. Why hadn't I left the room as soon as I identified Camille's perfume?

"You did it, didn't you?" I said, even as my brain screamed for me to keep my mouth shut. "You killed them."

Camille's eyes flashed, and she wiped her hands off on a cloth napkin. "You should be careful what you say. The truth has a nasty habit of biting back." She slid her hand down her leg and I took a step backwards.

"Listen, Camille, I don't know what's going on here, but I think it's best if we go rejoin the party." I held my hands up in front of me and glanced towards the door.

"Not so fast." She whipped her hand out from under her dress, her fingers curled around a gun.

My mouth went dry at the sight of the gun and I strained to keep from throwing up. My eyes darted to the door leading to the next room, where the party was still going on. Camille took a step closer to me.

"Oh, don't even think about it," she said, waving the gun in my face. "No way you make it to the door fast enough. We're going out the back way." She waved me to the glass doors on the other side of the room, which led to the property behind the inn. Where all the trees were.

"I guess my secret's out," she said, prodding me forward with the gun. "I killed Bethany, and now I'm going to have to kill you."

37

My whole body shook with each step. Somehow, I'd stumbled onto the killer, all because I'd wanted to help with some stupid macaroons. I continued walking to the back doors, trying to figure out how to get out of this.

Even with the band playing in the next room, there was still a decent chance someone would hear the gunshot and come find Camille. I'd be dead by that point, but at least she'd get arrested.

"Oh, wait, we can't forget the most important part," Camille said, grabbing a pillow from the couch in the room. "It'll muffle the sound of the gun," she explained, pleased with herself. "I learned that one from the TV. Can't have anyone hearing what's going on down here. Now move. And don't even think about screaming, or I'll shoot you before the first scream leaves your body."

We went out to the back area through the doors, dread sinking in as every moment passed. Goosebumps jumped up along my skin from the cold air.

"Why do you even have a gun on you?" I asked her, this new image of her struggling to make sense in my brain.

Camille laughed from behind me. "You never know when someone is going to figure out you're a killer. It never hurts to have a little protection with you. Keep moving."

I continued forward, stumbling over a rock, my mind racing a mile a minute. How was I going to get out of this? Camille had the gun trained on me the whole time, and I didn't know how good she was at using it. I could try to wrestle it from her, but that might lead to one of us getting shot, and I couldn't guarantee it wouldn't be me.

Maybe someone would step out the front door of the inn and hear us. I needed to keep her talking until I could come up with some kind of plan.

"Why are you doing this?" I asked. "Why did you kill Bethany?"

Camille smirked, leading me further into the woods. "I might as well tell you, it's not like you'll be around to tell anyone." We stepped over some rocks, the gun never once leaving my side.

"I loved Victor, way before Bethany ever did. He was so kind to me and so strong in his work. He...he didn't notice me or my feelings at first, but I knew I just needed more time for him to see me." Her face turned into a scowl. "But Bethany stole him from me. She decided one day she wanted him and went after him, using her mother's death as an excuse to get close to him. I'd been working in his office for weeks, trying to get him to see that I was the one he should be with, and she swooped in and stole him from me. She came to take me to lunch one day and saw Victor, and it was like something came over him. Some instant connection that I had never seen from him. She would do anything for him, and she took him from me."

A bird cawed from the sky, causing both of us to jump, but Camille recovered before me and motioned for me to keep walking.

"Bethany pretended she didn't know how I felt about him, even after they got married," Camille continued. "She paraded him around like a toy, waving him under my nose. No regard for my feelings or thinking about how I'd feel having to see this every day. I left the company, but I couldn't leave town, not after I'd committed to this event year after year. This stupid, vapid event, which was a silly excuse for Bethany to dress up and have everyone tell her how amazing she was. It was all a lie, just a chance for her to get the recognition she never got as a child. And it ate me up inside."

Deep into the woods now, the inn disappeared behind us. We climbed through the trees, neither of us wearing shoes meant for this kind of activity. I struggled to keep on my feet, knowing that if I fell down, she might just shoot me to get it over with.

"What about Angeline?" I asked, stalling. "Did you kill her too?"

I heard the smirk in Camille's voice, even if I couldn't see her face. "Angeline should've stayed out of what wasn't her business. I had told the police I was out of town on business when Bethany was killed. Angeline knew I didn't have any meetings planned that night since she had access to all of our calendars. Rather than going to the police and forcing me to have to lie again, she told me what she knew and threatened to expose me if I didn't pay her. We met at her house to talk about it. I didn't mean to kill her, I just got so mad and hit her with a paperweight. I had to leave quickly. I didn't think you'd be the one to find her body, but since Angeline lived alone and who knows when someone would've found her body, it at least put the attention elsewhere."

"Did you come after me in that truck too?" I asked.

"It seemed like my only option. You were asking too many questions, getting too close to the truth. I had to do something before you figured it out, but another car was coming around the bend and I couldn't get close enough to see if you were dead. Imagine my surprise when you showed up at the inn the next day. I knew it was too risky to try again."

"Why did you kill Bethany? Because she took the man you loved?"

"Because she was trying to get pregnant!" Camille cried. The woods were silent at her outburst, as if the trees and the birds and the little wood creatures understood the severity of what was happening. "She came to me and told me she and Victor were going to start a family, that they were finally ready to bring kids into this world, and I lost it! She'd stolen the only man I loved, and now she was going to make a family with him, and I couldn't handle it. I deserved Victor, not her. I'd spent so long trying to make him happy and showing him how great I was, and now she was going to give him something that I didn't have the chance to."

Camille was now sobbing, the impact of what she had done and what had led us here finally hitting her. The woods loomed around us, pressing down on us as we stumbled through the dark. I racked my brain, trying to think of a way to get away from her. Would anyone hear me if I screamed? Or would she shoot me before I had a chance to even open my mouth? Where was she taking me?

"Keep walking," she said, nudging me with the gun when I slowed my pace. "I told her to meet me at the inn. I didn't think anyone would suspect me when they found her at the inn, and if anyone saw me, I could explain that I was there for business with the charity auction. I knew Sylvia's office was always unlocked and that no one would bother us that late."

As long as she was talking, she wasn't shooting me. It almost felt like she needed to get these words out. "Why did you meet her there so late? Wouldn't it have been more suspicious for someone to see you skulking around at night?"

Camille rolled her eyes. "I had a meeting at work that ran long. I'm surprised she still agreed to meet me. She wasn't known for her late-night meetings. I almost called it off when I saw what time we'd have to meet, thinking maybe I could find some other way to get rid of her, but I knew I was running out of time. And now you are, too. Stop walking."

I did as she said, my legs wobbling beneath me as death hovered nearby. No way was I going to let this woman murder me after all the death she'd already caused. I didn't want to give up on the inn, and I didn't want to give up on myself. Remembering what Camille had said before about not being much of a runner, I thought there might be a chance for me to get out of this.

Taking a deep breath, I lunged backwards, kicking her in the stomach, and took off into the woods.

Camille cried out in pain and started chasing me. I was surprised she didn't shoot me, but I remembered the pillow and her wanting to keep it quiet. I darted through the woods, my heart pounding in my chest, my curls catching on tree branches as I ran away from a killer. So much for my hair not looking like a poodle.

My body warmed as I ran, and my mind cleared. I knew these woods well. I played in them every summer while I was a kid, and I could feel my memories of them returning. I bet Camille hadn't spent any time back here. I could run around to the front of the inn, but that was further away, and I didn't know if I'd get there quick enough.

Then I remembered: there was a pathway through the woods that led out to the road. I didn't think I'd make it to the road quick enough, and I didn't know if there would be any cars out this late, but if I could draw Camille out in that direction, maybe I could get the jump on her.

I headed in that direction, picking up my pace. All those mornings spent running were finally paying off. I broke out onto the pathway, relieved that I remembered where it was, then crouched down in the grass and weeds on the other side, waiting for Camille to come through.

She burst out through the woods, panting, the gun held out in front of her like a shield. She seemed surprised to see the pathway and waved the gun around, looking for me.

"Come out, come out, Simone," she said, her eyes wild and her hair a mess, frantically searching for me. "There's nowhere to go. Let's get this over with."

"Yes, let's," I whispered under my breath, then gave a lunge and tackled her. The gun flew out of her hands, into the woods, and I punched her in the face.

I sprang up and ran back towards the inn. I heard her scrambling in the bushes, trying to stand up. I only needed to get back to the inn, and then I would be safe.

Flashlight beams appeared in front of me, coming from all directions. A group of people pushed through the trees, bursting out in front of me. Detective Patel and Tracy were at the front. I ran over to them and almost knocked Tracy over with my hug. Finally, it was all over.

38

Two days later, I stood at the front desk, helping to check in a guest. The inn was quiet this morning, though we'd had a steady stream of guests ever since the charity auction. It seemed that attempted murder, actual murder, and fancy dresses did attract people to the inn. But I hoped we wouldn't make a habit of the murder part.

I'd kept quiet the past few days, staying up in my room reading and thinking about what I wanted to do with my life. I'd called Chrissy after everything had happened and told her what went down, needing to talk to someone who knew me and could let me vent. Of course, she'd wanted all the gory details.

"When are you coming home?" she'd finally asked once it was clear I didn't know enough to share with her.

"I'm not sure," I'd said, staring out my window to the woods in the back. Was I ever going to be able to look at those with the same happy memories I'd had as a kid? "I still have some things to take care of here."

After that call, I'd hung around the bistro a few times but hadn't talked to anyone about what had happened. I was still processing my near-death experience and thought I might break down if I tried to talk to anyone about it. Camille had scared me in those woods, and I wasn't going to look at them the same way for a long time.

However, today was the first day I'd woken up and felt ready to talk to others again. Nadia had seemed happy when I'd shown up at the front desk, though her enthusiasm was probably because she wanted a break.

Miles and Estelle came up to the front desk during a lull in guests. I hadn't seen them since the charity auction, and they were looking pleased with themselves. Lola hurried out from behind the desk to greet them and Miles slipped her a biscuit.

"We did it!" Miles said, holding his hand up for a high-five.

"Did what?" I asked, slapping his hand.

"Solved the murder! We're a real crime fighting team!" Estelle said, pumping her hand into the air. I smiled, wondering where they were when I'd been fighting off Camille. I was just grateful the police had shown up when they did.

"How did the police know where to find us?" I asked. "We were so far into the woods, I thought I was a goner."

"You don't know? Why, Damian went to Tracy," Estelle said. "He said he recognized Camille from some pictures Bethany had of her. Apparently, Bethany didn't have very positive things to say about Camille when they talked about her. This surprised Tracy since Camille always said such kind things about Bethany in public."

"Your detective, Patel?" Miles went on. "She'd come by

the inn with some officers because they'd figured out that Camille had lied about where she was when Angeline was killed and wanted to talk to her. Tracy remembered you saying you and Camille were working in the next room, but when they found it empty and the back door open, they all ran out into the night."

Estelle nodded. "Everyone was so scared when you weren't in that room anymore."

I was relieved to hear this. I'd been so scared out in the woods, certain I wouldn't make it. I hadn't expected anyone to save me, which is why I had to attack Camille myself.

"So Camille killed Bethany because she loved Victor that much?" Estelle asked.

"Who knows how much she actually loved Victor?" I said. "I think she just couldn't stand that Bethany had the life she wanted. When Bethany said they were going to try to have a family, it was too much for her."

I didn't quite understand the motive, but I could see how it could drive someone to murder. It also made me wonder if having a baby was the reason Bethany had been willing to let Damian into her life. Was she finally realizing the importance of family and wanting to make it work with him?

"What about Victor? Did Patel end up arresting him for anything?" I'd been so holed up in my room that I hadn't gotten any updates on anything.

Miles and Estelle's eyes opened wide in tandem, their surprise palpable. They glanced at each other, then back at me. "Have you not heard anything these past few days?" Miles asked. "Victor didn't kill his wife, but he was embezzling from his company! He was working on some shady deals. The police arrested him yesterday. His company is embarrassed and thinking about pulling ties out of Pine

Brook. The inn is getting enough business from the charity auction that I think they'll decide to stay since it's too good a place for business to leave yet. But they were mighty upset to hear about what's happened."

Wow, I couldn't believe it. Victor had been embezzling from his company? That explained why he was so upset when I first talked to him. He really was grieving for his wife.

But then, when Tracy was arrested for Bethany's murder, he was probably hoping the police would stop asking questions, which is why he didn't want to talk about her case anymore when I went to see him. And why he'd gotten so upset when I'd asked him about his whereabouts that night. He didn't want anyone to know he was stealing from his company.

I also remembered how he told me that the town wouldn't appreciate a newcomer poking around. Had he just been trying to keep me from learning about his embezzling?

So much had happened the past few days. It was a lot to take in. Fortunately, the inn was still standing.

"How was the rest of the charity auction?" I asked them. After confronting Camille and the cops arriving, I'd gone with the police to give my statement and, by the time I'd made it back to the inn, the charity auction was wrapped up.

"It was quite a hit!" Estelle said with a smile. "Even with all the murder. I think it's part of the reason the inn has seen so much business the past few days. Everyone wants to stay here now."

It was pretty amazing how many guests we now had. I was surprised when I'd shown up that morning, but we'd worked our way through everyone. Hank was doing really well in the kitchen, cooking up a storm, riding the high from how positive everyone had been about his food during the event.

All the rooms were booked up, and it was looking like I was going to have to find a new place to stay, because it made more sense to sell my room to a guest, rather than letting me stay in it for free.

Of course, that depended on how much longer I was going to be in town for, and I still didn't quite know the answer to that question. I wasn't ready to leave yet, but I still needed to talk to someone.

I stretched my back, appreciating the dull ache in my legs. After what had happened at the charity auction, I had been anxious about getting back outside and running again. But I'd grown to appreciate that time for myself, and I'd woken up this morning with an urge to run. Knowing that the person who had attacked me was in jail helped my nerves a lot.

Just then, the front door flew open and Tracy walked to the front desk. Estelle and Miles said their goodbyes and hurried back to the bistro, hoping to get some turnovers before Hank ran out. Tracy smiled at me as she came around the counter, putting her bag down in a cubby.

"How are you?" she asked, straightening up some papers.

"Not too bad," I said, unsure of where to put my hands or where to look. We hadn't had a chance to talk after she found me with Camille, and I found myself a bit tongue-tied. The inn had been doing well, which was great to hear, but I knew I needed to make a decision about what I was going to do.

"Listen, Tracy," I said, but she interrupted me.

"I'm sorry," she said, coming to stand in front of me.

"For what?"

"For how I treated you when you first showed up. Like I said, I was upset about Sylvia and didn't know what we were going to do with the inn, but I shouldn't have taken it out on you the way I did. You are a great asset to this place, and I know your aunt would've been so proud to see you here. She talked about you sometimes, did you know that? You and your sister. She loved you both and wished she could've seen you more often."

My eyes pricked up with tears at her words. I hadn't known that about Sylvia. I remembered the letter Sylvia had written me and realized then how much she did love me.

"Tony Vasco made another offer to me," I blurted out. I didn't know why I'd said it, but I didn't want to keep it from her.

Tracy's head shot up. "Really?"

I nodded. "At the auction. It was before everything got crazy with Camille."

"I guess that means you'll be heading back to California," Tracy said, turning away from me.

My heart sank. "Well, I'm not so sure about that," I said carefully. She looked up at me in surprise. "I actually told him no. I just... I've enjoyed being here. Well, ignoring the murder investigation and almost getting killed part. But I love this place, I loved it as a kid, and I think it's really special."

I'd been thinking about this for the past few days; my heart told me Aunt Sylvia would want us to do this together.

"If you'll have me, I'd like to say and help run the inn," I said, barely able to look her in the eye.

Tracy grinned, wider than I'd ever seen it. "I'd love that," she said. "Hopefully, we won't run into any more killers while you're here."

As we turned back to the front desk to help check a new guest in, I couldn't stop my grin. Looks like I now had an inn to run. If only we knew how prophetic Tracy's words were.

ENJOYED THIS BOOK?

If you enjoyed reading about Simone and the town of Pine Brook, I'd love it if you could leave a review. Honest reviews of my books help bring them to the attention of other readers. You can leave a review at the book's Amazon page.

Book 2 of the Hemlock Inn Mysteries, *College and Criminals*, is now available on Amazon! Grab your copy today.

ACKNOWLEDGMENTS

A book is a work of love, sweat, and tears, and so many helped me get to this point.

Thanks to Max for encouraging my passion, even when it meant I wouldn't watch Netflix with him. To Ashley for always supporting my stories. To Dimitra for her excellent feedback and encouragement. To Carmen for her insights; this book is so much stronger because of her. To Amber for holding my hand through the process. To Michele for inspiring a love of books at such a young age.

And to the rest of my friends and family, thank you for all your support and encouragement.

And to you, dear reader, for helping me to do what I love.

ABOUT THE AUTHOR

Josephine Smith is an author of cozy mysteries. A Washington state native, Josephine now makes her home in Northern California with her husband and dog and cat. She loves all things sweet, foods and people included, and can be found with her nose buried in a book. You can find her online at www.josephinesmithauthor.com, Facebook at www.facebook.com/josephinesmithauthor, and Instagram at www.instagram.com/josephinesmithauthor.

Made in United States
Orlando, FL
23 December 2023

41636980R00147